MW00757178

THE WILLOUGHBYS RETURN

THE WILLOUGHBYS RETURN

LOIS LOWRY

HOUGHTON MIFFLIN HARCOURT
BOSTON NEW YORK

hmhbooks.com

The text was set in Bembo Book MT Std.
Design by Natalie Fondriest

Library of Congress Cataloging-in-Publication Data
Names: Lowry, Lois, author.
Title: The Willoughbys return / by Lois Lowry.
Description: Boston : Houghton Mifflin Harcourt, [2020] |
Series: The Willoughbys | Audience: Ages 8 to 12. | Audience: Grades 4–6. | Summary: Thirty years after their disappearance, the previously frozen Willoughbys have thawed out and returned from the Alps, to the consternation of their children and grandchildren.
Identifiers: LCCN 2019058453 (print) | LCCN 2019058454 (ebook) |
ISBN 9780358423898 (hardcover) | ISBN 9780358423904 (ebook)
Subjects: CYAC: Family life—Fiction. |
Brothers and sisters—Fiction. | Humorous stories.
Classification: LCC PZ7.L9673 Wk 2020 (print) |
LCC PZ7.L9673 (ebook) | DDC [Fic]—dc23
LC record available at https://lccn.loc.gov/2019058453
LC ebook record available at https://lccn.loc.gov/2019058454

Manufactured in the United States of America
DOC 10 9 8 7 6 5 4 3 2 1
4500803384

FOR JAY AND ASHLEY

1

The front page of the *New York Times,* on a Thursday in June:

CONGRESS VOTES OVERWHELMINGLY TO BAN CANDY, CITES DENTAL HEALTH

On the same day, on an inside page of a Zurich newspaper:

AMERICAN COUPLE, FROZEN IN SWISS MOUNTAINS FOR THREE DECADES, THAW SPONTANEOUSLY, APPEAR UNHARMED

These two events, it was later proved, were related. It's complicated.[1]

[1] So pay attention. It will be confusing at first. But it's worth hanging in there. And there won't be a quiz.

2

High on a mountain in Switzerland (one of the Alps, though a minor Alp, not a particularly well-known Alp, not the Matterhorn or one of those postcard-y ones), an odd, lumpy, ice-encrusted shape began to move slightly, causing the glistening snow to shift.

It had been very warm and sunny for days. Weeks, actually—even months. Across the globe, glaciers had shrunk and icebergs had dissolved. Now, on this insignificant Alp, which had been snow-covered for eons, suddenly rocks began to appear, sleek with water from the snowmelt. Here and there a green stem emerged, and an occasional flower.

And now, a moving lump.

Then, beside the first strangely moving shape, another large, snowy lump shifted. Amazingly, from one of the shifting mounds, a hand emerged. It brushed some snow aside, revealing an entire arm. Then a second arm appeared.

The first mound sat up, and the two arms, moist

from the melted snow, began to brush snow and wipe water from a face. It was a newly defrosted face, male, with a glowering frown. It looked around, perceived the second mound nearby, and reached over to give it a poke. Then another poke, and another. Finally the second lump sat up, also frowning. This one appeared to be female (though it is hard to tell, with a lump).

"I bet anything my hair is an absolute mess," the second lump grumbled.

But the first lump paid no attention. He was testing his stiff fingers, tapping at them to dislodge a few ice particles. Finally he reached down to his right hip and removed a soggy wallet from his pocket.

"I knew it!" he groaned, prying open the wet leather. "My money is ruined! Sodden. Practically *dissolved.* And all stuck together in a messy wad."

"Our dollars?"

"No, those ridiculous Swiss francs[1] they made us get. Clearly inferior. American dollars wouldn't deteriorate like this."

"Well, are they usable enough for food, at least? I'm hungry."

[1] Most countries in Europe started using Euros in 1995. But not Switzerland. They still like their francs.

"Of course they'll take our money. They're all crooks here."

The woman (because they were a pair: man and woman) groaned, struggled to her feet, then knelt. "Where's my purse? I don't see my purse." On her hands and knees, she began pawing through the wet snow. "Here!" she said. "Here it is! But yuck—it's drenched!"

"Don't worry about it. And stand up! You look like a cockroach, crawling around that way. Come on. We'll make our way down to the village and get a quick lunch—not that they have any decent food in this godforsaken place. Then we'll get the first train out." The man stood upright with some difficulty and replaced the wet billfold in his hip pocket.

Finally the pair, grumbling and complaining, managed to stumble slowly down the side of the thawing Alp, passing on the low slopes meadows dotted with cows, toward the tiny village at its foot. The one main street was lined with brightly painted homes and dotted with flower boxes filled with petunias and geraniums. They found a table at a small café, where they ate heartily of a veal stew and each had three glasses of quite a good wine. But they were thwarted when the bill was brought to their table.

"I'm so sorry," the waiter said as he looked with dismay at the sodden mass of Swiss francs that the man offered him. "Ve can't accept vet money. But—"

"*Vet*? Good lord, man—can't you even say the word *wet*?"

"Apologies, sir. I vill try harder. Damp vould be okay, perhaps. But soggy vet is bad."

"Give them a credit card, dear," the woman suggested.

With a loud sigh the man pried a platinum card loose from his waterlogged wallet.

"I'm sorry, Mr. . . ." The waiter looked carefully at the card. "Ah, Mr. Villoughby. But this credit card expired many years ago."

"It's WILLOUGHBY, you idiot! Why can't you dolts pronounce a W the way normal people do?"

"I'm wery sorry, sir. I vish I could," the waiter replied, with a roll of his eyes that implied he did not vish any such thing.

The maître d' appeared, smiling politely. "Is there a problem?" he asked. Then he looked more closely at the ill-tempered couple. "Oh. I see you've defrosted. You're still damp."

"Defrosted?" bellowed Mr. Willoughby. "What on earth—"

"You were frozen," the maître d' explained, and peered at the date on the credit card. "And now you've thawed. It's happened to a number of climbers."

"And many goats, as vell," the waiter added. "It's the varming."

"The *vat?* I mean: *what?*"

"Global varming, sir."

Mrs. Willoughby sighed. "You never believed in that, Henry. But *now* look." She patted her own head. "My hairstyle is hopelessly out of date. Take me home, right away."

"Bring me a telephone," Mr. Willoughby demanded.

"Of course," the maître d' said. He nodded to the waiter, who scurried away to find a phone. "You must call your family."

"Family?" Henry Willoughby said, looking startled.

His wife groaned. "Oh lord, we have those horrible children. Do we know their phone number, Henry? Do we even know where they live?"

Her husband shrugged. "I forget. But we don't have to worry about them. We hired that nanny, remember?"

"Oh, yes. The nanny."

"Anyway, it doesn't matter about them," her husband muttered. "I'm calling my bank."

The maître d' smiled politely. "You should certainly do that," he said. "You owe us vun hundred and twelve Swiss francs for your dinner. I do hope you enjoyed the weal? And may I pour you some more of this vine?"

3

Sad to say, the nanny had passed away some years before. She was immortalized now in an oil portrait that hung in—

Oh, wait. A little history is necessary here. A little filling in of the details.

Many years before—thirty years to be exact—Mr. and Mrs. Willoughby had embarked on an extended vacation,[1] leaving their four children behind. They didn't like the children very much (and to be honest, the children didn't like them, either), and so it was not a tragedy for them to be separated. But it would have been illegal for them to leave the children all alone (the eldest, Tim, was just twelve). To keep things on the up-and-up, Mr. Willoughby had advertised for a nanny and had hired the no-nonsense woman, who ap-

[1] They used the Reprehensible Travel Agency. The company ceased operation some years ago after consistently bad reviews on Yelp.

peared at the front door on her first day of work with a starched and folded apron in her satchel.

Then, when their parents did not return (because they had stupidly worn shorts and sandals to go mountain climbing) and finally the Swiss government had announced that the couple had frozen solid on an Alp, perched on an icy ledge from which they could not be retrieved (though for a few coins they could be viewed by telescope from several tourist locations), and the house in which they had lived was sold, the children and Nanny had to rethink their living arrangements. Fortunately, Nanny was very enterprising. She took a job in the nearby home (mansion, actually) of a man, founder and president of Consolidated Confectionaries, Inc., who had made a fortune manufacturing candy. All four children, and even their cat, went with her.

And guess what! The billionaire, Commander Melanoff, fell in love with her! Well, why wouldn't he? She was a wonderful cook, a fine housekeeper, a no-nonsense woman, and a dutiful caretaker not only of the children but of Commander Melanoff himself. She trimmed his mustache and sprinkled cinnamon on his oatmeal. He was a very rich and very lonely bachelor. In time there was a wedding and a happily-ever-after.

Except—

Oh dear. Eventually, after many years, she passed away. And now she was an oil portrait hanging on the front wall of the mansion. Commander Melanoff had commissioned the portrait from a famous painter, and he had directed that the portrait show Nanny the way he fondly remembered her: with her no-nonsense expression, and oven mitts on her hands. He had installed special lighting so that she seemed to glow.

The commander, an elderly man now, lived in a palatial suite of rooms on the third floor. He spent his time reading history and composing poetry.[2] All of his poems were about Nanny. Whenever he was on the first floor, he stood in front of the portrait, gazing at it and reciting his odes to her memory.

Sometimes his grandson, eleven-year-old Richie, covered his ears and begged, "Not that one, Grandpa!" when the commander began to intone with reverence: "*There once was a woman named Nanny . . .*"

"That's inappropriate, Grandpa!" Richie said, because he knew the next line, which referred to Nanny's backside and began "*Who had an incomparable . . .*"

[2] So far he had composed seven sonnets, twenty-two haiku, and a nineteen-line villanelle. His favorite, though, was a limerick that was slightly naughty.

"Nothing is inappropriate if it is true," the commander replied, and continued his recitation. But Richie chanted *"La la la"* very loudly and ran off down the hall so that he couldn't hear the poem.

Oh, wait. We have to explain Richie. The Willoughby children had all grown up, of course. They had gone to college and taken jobs and moved away to live their various lives. All but Tim. Tim, the eldest, had always been a clever boy. Now forty-two years old, with the blessing of Commander Melanoff, he had taken over the candy manufacturing company, which had continued its enormous and profitable success. He and his wife lived in the mansion with their little boy. Richie was Tim Willoughby's son.

4

What's wrong?" Richie asked, entering the large dining room where his parents were having breakfast. "I can hear Grandpa sort of *yowling* up on the third floor."

Then he looked at his father, who had just crumpled the *New York Times,* had thrown it onto the floor, and was pounding the mahogany table with his fist. At the edge of his placemat, his coffee cup had overturned and a dark puddle of coffee was expanding.

At the other end of the table, Richie's mother rang the small silver bell that summoned the maid, who appeared instantly through an unobtrusive door.

"Clean that up, please, before it damages the rug," Ruth Willoughby directed the maid, indicating the spilled coffee with a nod of her head.

"And the paper, ma'am? Shall I smooth it out?" the maid asked, indicating the crumpled *New York Times* on the carpet. But Richie's mother murmured, "No, get rid of it." So the maid wiped up the spilled coffee, then collected the ruined newspaper and took it to the kitchen to add to the recyclables. (The Willoughby family, and Commander Melanoff as well, were all very environmentally aware.)

Tim Willoughby subscribed to the *New York Times* and the *Wall Street Journal*. But he had no reason, really, to read European newspapers, like the one in Switzerland that had recently described, in a brief article, the amazing reappearance of the defrosted couple in the Alps.

Too bad. He would have been very interested in that article, because the newly thawed Americans were his parents.

But he had been distracted by the major headline and front-page news from the US Congress. The banning of candy! How could this have happened? Well, he knew exactly how it had happened! It was the dentists! The American Dental Association! They had been lobbying for months against candy. They ran ads on TV showing openmouthed children displaying rotting, discolored teeth while the voice of a mournful dentist explained gloomily how if only they had not eaten candy, they would not have reached this sad state.

And finally all of the senators and representatives had been convinced. Well, not *all*. An elderly Democratic senator from Vermont, a bald man with ill-fitting false teeth and a liking for gummy bears, had voted against the bill. And there were two Republicans who had found it amusing to show up on the floor of the House of Representatives sucking on lollipops. They had also voted no.

But they were the only ones. And now, with the candy-ban bill voted into law, the newspaper said, candy was to be immediately removed from stores across the country. Factories would be closed down. Halloween trick-or-treating would be reworked—maybe comic books could become the new treats?

Richie was still standing in the doorway when his grandfather, wearing a bathrobe, came down the long stairway. He was no longer yowling, but he was snuffling and dabbing at his eyes. At the foot of the stairs he turned, as he always did, and bowed his head in front of Nanny's portrait. Richie cringed, hoping his grandpa would not begin to recite a naughty poem. But Commander Melanoff only murmured, "Nanny, Nanny, Nanny . . ."

Then he turned, patted Richie briefly on the head, and entered the dining room. "You've heard?" he asked Tim.

"Yes," Richie's father replied in a low voice.

"We're ruined, aren't we?"

Tim Willoughby nodded. "Ruined. Totally."

In the silence that followed, Richie asked, "Is it okay if I go out and play?"

His father stared at him. "What do you plan to play with?"

Richie thought. "Um, my Firepulse Innovation top-grain leather basketball."

"Is that new?" his father asked.

"Yes. I ordered it last week and it just came yesterday. I'm not sure if I like it yet. I might get a Spalding TF-1000."

Richie had always been allowed to order whatever toys or gadgets he wanted. Billionaires (and their children, and even their grandchildren) can do that, of course.

His father rose from his seat, went to his son, and put his arm around him. "Richie, we're going to have to cut back."

"Huh?"

"You go ahead outside to play with your basketball. But don't order anything else. We're destitute. We've been destroyed."

"Destroyed?"

"Yes. By dentists."

5

In the well-tended yard (gardeners clipped and mowed and trimmed constantly) of the mansion, Richie bounced[1] his new basketball half-heartedly and thought briefly about dentists. But his thoughts were boring, and he hadn't completely understood when his father said they'd have to cut back. He had thought it referred to the shrubbery.

He pushed aside the thick rhododendron bushes that grew beside the fence and glanced into the yard next door to see if the Poore children might be playing there. The aptly named Poores had no lawn, no bushes, no landscaping—nothing but sparse grass and weeds around their tiny house.

But the yard next door was empty. Richie sighed. He bounced his ball again a few times. Inside the man-

[1] He should not have done this. A top-grain leather basketball is intended for indoor use only. But Richie hadn't read the instructions.

sion, his father and grandfather were talking urgently on the phone to banks, to corporate headquarters, to the dispatcher who monitored the location of all fourteen hundred trucks that carried candy around the country and even into Canada. It was all illegal now: all those thousands of chocolate bars and lollipops and chewy caramels. And licorice sticks! Oh my! It was their best seller, had been for decades: the thin, rubbery spiraled candy called Lickety Twist.

6

In the little house on the other side of the fence, where it sat in the shadow of the mansion, Mrs. Poore and her children were in the kitchen.

The Poore children had never tasted Lickety Twist. They had never tasted any candy at all because they were . . . well, poor.

They were, at this moment, seated at their kitchen table finishing their breakfast of gruel.[1] It was what they had every morning. Lunch each day was watery soup with some sliced potatoes and occasionally a carrot. Dinner was always stew; sometimes there was a chunk of unidentifiable meat in it.

"The Fourth of July won't be the Fourth of July without fireworks," Winifred Poore, age ten, announced loudly, stirring her gruel.

"What are you talking about?" asked her twelve-

[1] Gruel is a disgusting porridge-y thing, sort of like oatmeal but much, much worse: watery, and full of lumps.

year-old brother, Winston (their parents, naming the children, had tried for a Win-Win situation). "It's only June."

"I know what month it is. I was just practicing talking like Jo, in *Little Women*. I have borrowed *Little Women*[2] from the library seventeen times. I like Jo best. She does a lot of grumbling about being poor, though. She says Christmas won't be Christmas without any presents. There aren't any presents because they're poor. Like us. And their father is gone, like ours."

Mrs. Poore took a folded tissue from her apron pocket and held it briefly to her eyes. "I do miss your father very much. But he's hard-working, and he—"

"You sound so much like Marmee, in the book." Winifred told her. "Maybe I'll start calling you Marmee."

"Please don't," said Mrs. Poore. "I prefer Mother."

"Well, you were Marming."

"What does that mean?"

[2] By Louisa May Alcott, published in 1868. There have been many movies of *Little Women*. The mother, Marmee, has been played by Spring Byington in 1933, Mary Astor in 1949, and Susan Sarandon in 1994. Laura Dern is the newest (2019) Marmee.

"Oh, talking in a pathetic way, kind of sweetly but in a way that makes people want to gag."

Winston looked up from his gruel and did a brief gagging imitation. Then he asked, "Where *is* Father? I mean, where is he now? I know we got a postcard from Ohio, but that was weeks ago."

(Their father, Ben Poore, had been gone for quite a long time. He was an encyclopedia salesman. He held the world record, actually, for sales. He had never sold a single one.)

Mrs. Poore sighed. "Poor Father," she said. "He had a difficult time in Ohio. He's gone farther west. He's now—"

"I'm fond of Ohio," Winifred commented. "It has an O at each end."

"Why did he have a difficult time?" Winston asked. He stood up to take his empty gruel bowl to the sink.

His mother sighed. "Well, he was going door to door, as he does, with his encyclopedia samples, and—"

Winston groaned. "Those stupid encyclopedias," he said. "He tried to sell a set to my sixth grade teacher, but she looked at it and said it was way out of date."

"That's why the price is so reasonable," his mother explained.

"But you can't look up, say, computers in an encyclopedia that was published before they were invented," Winston pointed out.

"Or the newest elements," Winifred added. Winifred was very interested in science. "I don't think Father's encyclopedia has any elements since, oh, probably Bohrium.[3] And there are something like eleven more after that."

Mrs. Poore sighed. "Well, look up Abe Lincoln instead, then. Or steam engines."

"Or granite," Winifred said. Geology was Winifred's favorite scientific study. She collected rocks. Granite was her favorite.

"Why did Father have a difficult time in Ohio?" Winston asked again.

"Well," his mother explained, "he opened the gate to a yard, intending to knock on the door of the house, and a dog bit him." She paused. "And I'm sorry to say that he kicked the dog."

Winifred gasped. "Father *kicked a dog?*"

"Well, yes, he did. I'm sure it was a very vicious dog. But Father was arrested for animal abuse. The au-

[3] Atomic number 107, Bohrium is named after the Danish physicist Niels Bohr. It has a half-life of about one minute.

thorities finally let him go, but he had to agree to leave town. So he headed west."

Mrs. Poore stirred her tea, then carefully lifted the teabag out of her cup and examined it. "I think I can get at least two more breakfasts out of this bag," she said, and set it aside carefully. "Thrift is a great virtue, children. Remember that."

"Marming," murmured Winifred, and her brother nodded in agreement.

Mrs. Poore ignored the murmur and turned to her daughter. "Are you fond of any state with vowels on either end?" she asked. "Like Idaho and Indiana? Or does it have to be the same vowel?"

Winifred thought. "Same," she said.

Her mother smiled and sipped. "In that case, you'll be fond of Father's current location. "He's in Alaska now."

"Alaska?" Winston asked. "Why Alaska?"

"He felt quite certain that they would need encyclopedias in Alaska. And in between door-to-door sales calls, he thought he might try prospecting for gold," Mrs. Poore explained.

"Gold would be nice," Winifred said. She stood and placed her bowl in the sink next to her brother's. "They discovered gold around 6000 BCE. The woman next door? She has a gold bracelet. Sometimes she comes outside to call to her son, and I can see it all shimmery on her arm."

Mrs. Poore sighed a little and looked at her own bare wrist.

"Sorry," Winifred said. "I probably shouldn't have mentioned it."

"Does Father know how to do that?" asked Winston with a dubious look. "Prospecting?"

"He planned to look it up in the encyclopedia," his mother explained. "He sent me a postcard, just a few sentences, last week. The scenery was nice, he said, but he was cold. He wondered if I would knit him a scarf."

"Did you?" asked Winifred.

"No, dear. Yarn is too expensive."

Winifred began to cry. "Poor Father," she wept.

"Do we have any tissues?" she whimpered, after a moment. "My nose is dripping."

"Just this one, into which I recently sneezed," her mother answered, taking it from her apron pocket. "Tissues are so expensive. Here you go."

"Never mind," Winifred said. "I guess I'll use my sleeve."

7

At the very moment that Winifred Poore was wiping her drippy nose on her sleeve, her father, Ben Poore, was sound asleep in southeast Alaska. It was four hours earlier there.

The afternoon before, he had been to the local post office in Whitehorse to mail a gift to his daughter.

"How's it goin'?" the postal clerk had asked.

Ben Poore had sighed. "Not very well," he told the clerk. "The soles of my shoes are wearing thin. I'm having zero luck selling encyclopedias. And my samples are heavy to carry around. I don't suppose you'd be interested? I could give you a special price . . ."

The clerk gave an impatient sigh. "I *meant:* How's it *goin'?* Priority? Overnight? Parcel Post?" She picked up the clumsily wrapped package he had placed on the counter. "Yikes. That weighs a ton. What've you got in there—*rocks?*"

Ben Poore was startled. "How did you know that? Are you a mind reader or what?"

"Just a guess."

"Well," he said, "good guess. I'm sending Alaskan rocks to my daughter. She loves— Whaddya call it? *Geology*, that's it. She wants to be a geologist. So I'm sending her a bunch of rocks."

The clerk weighed the package. "Well, it's gonna cost you thirty-two dollars to send it the cheapest way. And it'll take a while to get there."

He winced. "No rush. But thirty-two dollars? I'm running low on cash," he confided. "If I don't sell a set of encyclopedias soon . . ." He interrupted himself. "Hey! I bet the M volume has a lot of information about mind reading! How about—"

"Nope. Sorry." She held out her hand for the money.

Reluctantly he took two twenty-dollar bills from the thin roll of cash he had left and gave them to her. She counted out his change.

"I was going to stop in that café down the street for supper," Ben Poore said, pocketing the bills. "But now I can't afford it. I guess I'll just get myself a candy bar."

The clerk. "No, you won't. Haven't you heard the news?"

"What news?"

"Candy's illegal now. New law."

"Illegal?"

"Jail time."

"I can't even buy a Milky Way? Or a Nestlé Crunch bar?"

"White-collar crime."

"Even M&M's?"

"All candy," she said.

"What if someone gives me a really expensive box of Godiva chocolates?"

She stared at him, with his unkempt beard and coffee-stained plaid shirt. Briefly she glanced over at the post office wall, to the Most Wanted posters tacked there, and decided he wasn't a match. But she chose not to comment on the Godiva chocolates.[1] Instead, she beckoned to the person behind him in line. "Next?" she called.

"Jeez. Well," he said, turning to leave the post office, "I'll make do with an apple, I guess."

"Good for your teeth!" she called after him.

[1] Assorted Gold Gift Box, 105 pieces, $150.00. Worth every penny.

8

The Poores were unaware, of course, that their absent father had mailed a package to his daughter the day before, or that Mr. and Mrs. Willoughby had made their way back from Switzerland and would soon arrive in the same neighborhood where they lived. The Willoughby house, an old-fashioned four-story residence that had been their home before they left on their ill-fated vacation, was just a few blocks away.

No one called it the Willoughby house, though. Everyone had forgotten who had once lived there—that it had been an ill-tempered banker and his equally ill-tempered wife, along with their four children. Tim Willoughby, on his way to and from the confectionary factory, always had his chauffeur take a different route so that he didn't have to glimpse the house and remember his boyhood years. When they became adults, he and his siblings had created a fund that memorialized Henry and Frances Willoughby by supporting good causes of various kinds. But the sad truth is they had never really missed the ill-tempered couple who had gone on a vacation without them and been turned into human popsicles on an Alp thirty years before.

And the Poores? They had never heard of the Willoughbys. The only neighbors that interested the Poore children were the people who lived next door, Richie and his parents—and his grandfather—in the mansion. Winifred and Winston were fascinated by the sprawling giant of a house with its turrets and balconies and even gargoyles.[1]

Winifred Poore had counted the mansion's windows several times. The number was always the same: thirty-seven.

"We only have six windows," she had sighed one afternoon. "And they have thirty-seven."

"Think of it as an opportunity for reviewing math," her brother had suggested. "Thirty-seven minus six equals . . ."

[1] Gargoyles, which are meant to divert water, have been around for a long time. In the twelfth century, Saint Bernard of Clairvaux didn't like the gargoyles on his monastery. "What is the meaning of these unclean monkeys, these strange savage lions, and monsters? To what purpose are here placed these creatures, half beast, half man, or these spotted tigers?" he wrote.

"I don't have enough fingers for that."

"You're not supposed to count on your fingers," Winston pointed out. "What if you didn't have fingers? A lot of poor people don't."

"Why not?" asked Winifred. "Why don't they? Fingers don't cost anything. You don't have to *buy* fingers."

"Of course you don't. But poor people have to work in factories with dangerous machinery. So their fingers get chopped off." Her brother, with a grin, held up one hand with two fingers folded it over so it looked as if they were missing.

Winifred shuddered. But she picked up her pencil and did the math problem on the back of a torn piece of newspaper. "Thirty-one," she said. "They have thirty-one more windows than we do. It isn't fair."

"Of course it isn't fair," Winston agreed. "But we should—" He hesitated, looking at his mother and sister meaningfully until they both chimed in.

"Make the best of it." It was something the family often said. When Father had come home looking gloomy and said, "I didn't sell a single set of encyclopedias, and I stepped in a mud puddle and ruined my only pair of shoes," they said it. When dinner was nothing more than a thin beige stew with a few limp carrots and a bruised

potato, they said it. And now, when Winifred sulked about the comparison of windows, they said it again.

"What exactly does that mean, to make the best of it?" Winifred asked.

"I don't know," her brother replied.

Mrs. Poore smiled as she stood at the sink wiping the cereal bowls with a ragged dishtowel. "It means, dear, that some people, like us, live in tidy little houses and count our pennies and eat gruel for breakfast. But we don't complain. And we don't envy others."

"You're Marming, Mother," Winston pointed out.

"Sorry."

"You mean don't envy Richie next door? Who has thirty-seven windows? And probably Belgian waffles with real maple syrup for breakfast?" Winifred asked gloomily.

"Exactly. We must feel happy for Richie."

"Oh, Mother," Winifred sighed, "you are *such* a Marmee."

* * *

Wandering into their yard after breakfast, Winifred and Winston watched through the fence as Richie bounced his basketball a few times, then set it carefully on the porch. He went inside and returned after a moment with a large toy car. Winston glanced down at the chipped, three-wheeled toy car in his own hand. His father had carved it for him. Winston was fond of his little car, but now he deposited it on the ground and moved closer to the fence to see the amazing device that Richie had just set on the lawn.

"Wow! Is that yours, Richie?" he called.

"Yes. It's a remote-controlled replica of the exclusive Lamborghini Veneno Roadster," Richie replied.

"Did you have a birthday?" Winifred asked, coming closer to the fence herself, though she wasn't terribly interested in cars.

Richie looked surprised. "No," he said. "I just saw it online, and so I ordered it." Then he added, "I'm not allowed to do that anymore. Because of dentists."

"What did dentists do?" Winifred asked.

"I'm not sure. Something. And now we're destitute."

"What does that mean?" Winifred asked.

"It means ruined."

"Ruined how?" asked Winston.

"I don't know," Richie replied.

"Well, you still have this fabulous car," Winston reminded him.

"Yeah," Richie said, and looked down at it. "The steering wheel controller's on the porch. It has a forty-nine-foot range, plays revving motor sounds through its integrated speaker, and guides the model in all directions, accelerating it to a maximum five point six miles per hour." He leaned down, checked the positioning of the car, then went to the porch and activated the controls. The car moved across the neatly trimmed grass, then made a U-turn, came back to its original starting point, and stopped. "The iconic Lamborghini bull adorns the hubcaps and hood, the LED head- and taillights illuminate, and the exterior is painted the same shade as the full-size version," Richie recited.

He sent the vehicle around the yard again. Then he came down from the porch, picked up the car, and went back into his mansion.

The Poore children turned away from the fence and sat side by side in their unkempt yard. Winston picked up his little toy car and maneuvered it in and out among some weeds, carefully avoiding a line of ants moving in meticulous order toward their anthill.

"If we had a computer, we could order things," he grumbled.

"If we had money, we could get a computer," Winifred replied.

"If Father had a real job, we'd have money," Winston pointed out.

There was a long silence while they felt a little guilty for criticizing Father. He was a kind man and it wasn't his fault that no one wanted outdated encyclopedias.

Finally Winifred said, "If *we* had jobs, we'd have money."

"But who would hire us? Who *needs* us? We're useless." Winston poked at the ants with a twig and forced them to rearrange their tidy marching line.

Winifred considered that. Then she nodded toward the mansion on the other side of the fence. "I think maybe *he* needs us," she said.

"Who?"

"Richie. He's lonely."

9

At that very moment, Henry and Frances Willoughby were actually quite nearby. Just a few blocks away from the Poores, and the mansion next door to the Poores, the ill-tempered and oddly dressed (before they left Switzerland the American embassy[1] had provided them with clothing, but it didn't fit and was mostly brown) couple was standing on the sidewalk, complaining to anyone who would listen. There were not many listeners around, but Mr. Willoughby accosted a young woman pushing a stroller on the sidewalk and began to describe the situation until the toddler in the stroller wailed because he had dropped his pacifier. Mr. Willoughby, who disliked toddlers, especially wailing ones,

[1] U.S. Embassy, Sulgeneckstrasse 19, 3007 Bern, Switzerland. Go there if you lose your passport. Or become defrosted unexpectedly.

turned away and the woman walked hastily on. Next he called to a man driving a delivery truck. The truck slowed, and the driver lowered his window and called, "What?"

"This house!" Mr. Willoughby said. He indicated the tall house where his wife was standing at the foot of the front steps. "It used to be my house!"

"Great," the truck driver said. He revved his engine.

"But the people inside said they've never even heard of me!" Mr. Willoughby bellowed.

"I never heard of you either, mister," the truck driver said. He raised his window.

"My name is Henry Willough—"

The truck issued a small fart of gray smoke, moved forward, and disappeared around the corner.

"Or me!" his wife said in a petulant voice. "What about *me?*"

A squirrel, halfway up the trunk of a tree on the edge of the sidewalk, paused, tilted its head, and looked at the angry couple. Then, like the truck driver, it continued on.

"Ring the bell again," Mr. Willoughby commanded. "This is outrageous." His wife shifted her heavy purse[2] from her right arm to her left, mounted the steps, and pushed on the doorbell. Nothing happened. She pushed again and again until finally the red door jerked open and a heavyset man appeared.

"I told you! Quit bothering us! We're watching a ball game."

Mr. Willoughby began using his bank vice president voice: a quiet one oozing with politeness but with a thin, hostile edge to it. "Allow me to introduce myself. I'm Henry H. Willoughby. And you, sir, would be . . . ?"

The man, who had half closed the door, hesitated, because a hostile, oozing-with-politeness voice can be a little unnerving. "O'Leary," he said, after a pause. "Name's O'Leary."

"Delighted to meet you, Mr. O'Leary. You say you bought this house some years ago? Lovely house, by the way."

"Twelve years ago. I bought it from a guy named Rosenbaum. My kids were little when we moved in.

[2] She had recovered it, finally, from the wet snow, but it had been thoroughly soaked. Now, days later, the leather remained weighted and damp and was beginning to smell of mold.

Now they're teenagers. Got any idea what that's like, Willoughby? Three teenagers in the house?"

"I'm afraid I do not. The children are all, ah, *yours?*"

"Excuse me?"

"I meant, ah, you didn't acquire any children when you bought the house, by any chance?"

The man in the doorway stared at him. "The house was empty of children when we moved in. It will be empty of children again in four years, but who's counting, right? It will even be empty of the one who has twice been suspended from school for—"

"Knock it off, Dad." A tall teenage boy appeared, suddenly, in the doorway beside Mr. O'Leary. "The Yankees are ahead now, three to two. You missed a double." He glanced down at the strange pair: the frowning woman standing by the doorbell, and the man at the foot of the steps, whose face had turned quite pink with suspicion.

"Your name isn't by any chance Tim, is it?" Mr. Willoughby asked the boy. (Tim Willoughby, of course, was the son he had left behind.)

"No. Brian."

"Or Barnaby?" the woman asked, leaning forward to examine his face. "No, you don't look like a Barnaby." (Two of the other Willoughby children had been twins, both named Barnaby.[3])

"Who *are* these people, Dad?" the boy asked his father.

"I don't know. Their name is Willoughby and I guess they used to live here." Mr. O'Leary turned to the Willoughbys. "Good luck. I'm going back to my game now." He reached to close the door.

His son interrupted him. "There's a guy named Willoughby a few blocks away. In that mansion. You know the one, Dad? It was in all the papers when the old guy retired, because he was a billionaire?"

Mr. O'Leary frowned. "His name wasn't Willoughby. He had some weird foreign name."

"No, the guy who took over the company. He lives there now. I remember from when I delivered papers."

"You mean back when you were willing to work? Before you decided a summer job was beneath you?" his father asked him.

"A mansion! A mansion containing a Willoughby? We must go there, Henry," Mrs. Willoughby ordered her husband. *"Now."*

[3] This is unusual but not unheard of. The famous boxer George Foreman had five sons and named them all George.

Brian O'Leary gave them directions, pointing to the end of the block and describing the streets on which they should turn.

"Is it far?" Mrs. Willoughby asked as she joined her husband on the sidewalk. "My feet hurt."

"Take an Uber," Mr. O'Leary suggested. He pushed his son inside, turned away, and pulled the door closed behind himself.

"What's an Uber?" Mrs. Willoughby asked her husband.

"I have no idea," he told her. "It's probably a German swear word."

Grumbling to each other, they began to walk.

10

The defrosted Willoughbys were making their way toward the mansion very slowly, because Mrs. Willoughby's ridiculous high-heeled shoes didn't fit properly, and because Mr. Willoughby insisted on examining every parked car that they passed. None of them looked the way he thought an automobile should look. "Tesla?"[1] he said loudly. "What on earth is a Tesla?"

At that same moment, the Poore children were arguing with their mother in the kitchen of their little house. "Whatever do you mean, you're going to apply for jobs? My dear children shouldn't have to go out and work," she said, and picked up a corner of her apron to wipe a tear away.

"But we need food, Mother," Winston pointed out.

"And new clothing," Winifred added, demonstrat-

[1] C'mon. You know what a Tesla is, even if they don't. It's an electric car. The first one appeared in 2008.

ing with a gesture to her outfit, which was much too small.

"And a computer," muttered Winston. He muttered because he knew his mother would not take kindly to that particular need. Fortunately she didn't hear him. She had gone to the broom closet and removed the broom, which was so deteriorated that it had only a few straw bristles. Nonetheless, despite the inadequacy of the broom, she began to sweep the kitchen floor.

"You're quite right," she said. "We do need money. And I have had an idea." She leaned down and tried to smooth the edge of a piece of linoleum that had cracked and torn loose. "I think it will provide for our needs until your father returns with his fortune."

"What is your idea, Mother?" Winifred asked.

"We will become a B-and-B," Mother announced.

"A *what?*" The two astonished Poore children spoke together.

"A B-and-B." Mother propped the broom against the side of the stove. "We simply need to do a little decorating. Winston, I want you to go to the storage closet immediately. Father's encyclopedias are all there, of course. But also, you'll find a leftover can of blue paint. I want you to touch up the shutters.

"And we'll hang my old straw hat on the front door. Hats on doors is a very B-and-B thing."[2]

"But, Mother," Winifred said, "you do know what B-and-B stands for, don't you? Bed-and-breakfast."

"Of course, dear. Guests will use my bed and I'll share yours. Would that be all right? We'll be very cozy all cuddled up. We can tell each other stories in the dark."

Winifred cringed. "Mother, you're Marming again. And what about breakfast?" she asked.

"What about it? Move your foot, dear. You're standing on some mouse poo."

"Well, our breakfast is always just, ah, you know . . . gruel." Winifred moved to the side so that her mother could attack the hardened mound with her dishrag.

"Hand me something to scrape with, Winston. It's always so difficult to get this loose. I thought that in the summer heat it might have softened." His mother took the kitchen knife that her son handed her and began to pry at the edges of the mound. "As for breakfast? We'll find a way to fancy up the gruel a bit. Maybe raisins?"

[2] Teddy bears, dried flowers, and antique baby clothes are also frequently part of B-and-B décor. But the Poores didn't have those.

That dark pellets loosened and scattered themselves on the floor. Mrs. Poore stood up, pleased with her efforts. "There," she said. "I'll just sweep those up."

11

Far, far away, in a sparsely populated area of western Canada, a pickup truck pulled to the side of the road and stopped briefly. Ben Poore climbed down from the passenger seat, then reached in to take his heavy backpack, reflecting briefly that he was glad to have mailed the package of rocks. At least he didn't have to carry that with him. He had saved only two; they lay in the bottom of his backpack, and now and then he glanced at them, reminding himself of how happy his children, especially Winifred, would be with the gift.

He looked up at the jagged mountains nearby. They were very beautiful, but he didn't notice because he had been looking at mountains for weeks now, and they were all very beautiful, but he was tired of them. Above the mountains, he realized, black clouds were forming.

"Sorry I can't take you any farther," the driver told him. "Hope you get a ride before the rain starts."

"You sure you don't want to buy a set of encyclopedias? Last chance. Big discount."

"Don't ask me that again, mister. I already said no."

"Sorry. Where I am, exactly?"

"Just outside Smithers," the driver said.

"Does Smithers have a school?" he asked. Schoolteachers always seemed interested in encyclopedias. No schoolteacher had ever bought one, but they always looked with interest at his samples.

"Beats me. Guess it must," the driver said.

"How far to Seattle?"

"Close to eight hundred miles." The driver revved his engine. "What'd you say your name was?"

"Poore. Ben Poore."

"Good luck to you, Mr. Poore." The driver slammed the door and drove off in a cloud of exhaust fumes.

Ben Poore slapped away a mosquito, wrestled his heavy pack onto his shoulders, and began to walk. He had started out in Anchorage, had been hitching rides now for four days, and was very tired.

Briefly, trudging along, he considered how he might lighten his load. Throw away the sample encyclopedia volumes, maybe? But (he was an optimist) he might still use them to make a big sale! Instead he should probably throw out the last of the weird-colored rocks that he'd been lugging around ever since he'd picked them up out of the water in Mineral

Creek,[1] back in Alaska. He sighed. He had already mailed most of them, and these last two were down at the very bottom of the pack; he'd have to take out all the books in order to find them. A nuisance. Anyway, they were pretty, with their shiny streaks. Maybe they'd bring him good luck. Or at least another ride before the rain began.

[1] A little geography lesson: Mineral Creek is a ten-mile-long creek flowing out of the Chugach Mountains from Mineral Creek Glacier, down a narrow valley in southwest Alaska.

12

According to the directions they'd been given, Mr. and Mrs. Willoughby were very close to the Melanoff mansion, where, they'd been told, someone named Willoughby now lived. But when they passed a small park with some benches on its periphery, Mrs. Willoughby begged her husband to let her sit down.

"I'm all sweaty," she said. "and my hair is a mess. And look! I'm getting a blister!" She wrenched off one of the too-small high-heeled shoes and showed him an inflamed place on her foot. He looked at it with distaste.

"You've never had attractive feet," he commented.

"I'm rubber, you're glue, everything you say bounces off me and sticks back on you," his wife chanted.

Henry Willoughby didn't reply. How could he? There was no reply to that. Ignoring his wife, he picked up a folded newspaper that someone had left on the bench. Behind them, some teenage boys kicked a soccer ball around on some mowed grass. A missed return sent the ball off the playing field, and a player chased it to where it had landed near the bench where the Willoughbys sat.

"Sorry, sir," the boy said, as he bent to retrieve the ball.

"Quite all right," Mr. Willoughby said in his dignified banker voice. "Good game? Not going to blow it the way Argentina did?"[1] He gave a hearty laugh, trying to sound athletic and masculine.

"What?" The boy looked confused.

"One to nothing, right? West Germany won it with a penalty kick!"

"What's West Germany?" The boy asked, looking puzzled for a moment. "I could Google it, I guess," he added. Then he tossed the ball toward his teammates and jogged over to the field.

Henry Willoughby leaned back on the bench. His shoulders were slumped. "*Google it*? I don't know what anyone is talking about," he complained. After a moment he looked at the newspaper he was still holding.

[1] West Germany won the 1990 FIFA World Cup, 1–0 over Argentina. Shortly thereafter, Germany was reunited into a single country and West Germany ceased to exist.

"And this print is too small. If only I hadn't lost my glasses on that dratted Alp!" He moved the paper closer to his face and squinted at the text.

"Oh my lord," he groaned suddenly, and turned to his wife, who was continuing to rub her swollen foot. "Frances?"

"What?" She was a little terse, still annoyed about his previous remark about her feet. She thought her feet were quite attractive, actually, if you didn't look at the blister.

"Look at this!" he said, and pointed to the newspaper. "We're in serious trouble."

"Why? Aside from my foot. And if I can just get some Band-Aids and better shoes, my foot'll be all right."

"Not your stupid foot. It's us, both of us. We're in the wrong year."

"What on earth are you talking about? And my foot isn't stupid."

"We went on that vacation. Remember? With the Reprehensible Travel Company?"

"Of course I remember. There was the helicopter over the volcano, and the kayaking among crocodiles, and then the—"

He interrupted her. "How old were we?"

"Oh lord, I'm not good at math. We had those children. The oldest—what was his name?"

"Tim."

"Yes, Tim. Dumb name. I can't imagine why we chose it. Anyway, he was twelve when we went off. And he was born when I was twenty-four. That means I was . . . Help me here. You're the banker. You're supposed to be good at numbers."

"That means you were thirty-six when we took the vacation. I would have been thirty-seven."

"Okay. So what?"

"Well, look at us."

Frances Willoughby was accustomed to doing whatever her husband told her to do. So she stared at him.

"How old do I look?" he asked, sitting up straight and pulling his shoulders back and his stomach in.

She shrugged. "Thirty-seven, I guess. How about me?"

"You're a little broad in the beam," he told her, "like a hippo. But you look thirty-six."

"So?" She began to try to wedge her foot back into the shoe. "Why are we in serious trouble?"

"Don't you *get it?*" he wailed. "Look at the date on

this paper! It's thirty years later! We were frozen for thirty years!"

Mrs. Willoughby looked very puzzled. "What?"

"We're supposed to be in our late sixties! Close to seventy!"

His wife thought about that. Then, suddenly, she smiled. "So all the women I knew back then—like Margaret Simpson, remember her? I played bridge with her, and she cheated? And Elaine Cohen, across the street? Always gossiping? And the horrible PTA mothers? All of them—they're almost seventy now?"

"Yes," her husband said.

"And I'm not? I mean, *we're* not?"

"That's right."

She leaned back and began to chortle.

"Don't be so gleeful," her husband said.

"Why not? They need face-lifts and I don't. Ha ha on them!"

"Here's the problem, Frances. Our children."

"Them? Tim and . . . the others. I forget their names."

"There were twins."

"Yes, that's right, Barnaby A and Barnaby B. It wasn't fair that they looked alike. I could never tell them apart. Oh, and . . . now I'm remembering. Didn't we also have a girl? She whined all the time."

Mr. Willoughby's facial expression softened. "Jane," he said, and sighed. "I liked Jane."[2]

"You're a sucker for whiners. Anyway, what's the problem with the children, aside from the fact that I suppose we have to be parents again, and it was never much fun?"

"The problem is this: They're no longer children," her husband said. "They're our age. Or *older*."

"Oh," Frances Willoughby replied. "My goodness. How strange. But we won't have to take care of them. I'm glad of that, at least."

"I'm afraid they'll have to take care of *us*," Mr. Willoughby said, gritting his teeth. "They've inherited our money."

There was a long silence. Then Mrs. Willoughby struggled to her feet, wincing a bit. "Well," she said, "let's find them, then. Because I need new shoes."

[2] Jane had grown up to be a professor of feminist studies in San Francisco. The twins, who lived in the Midwest, had changed their names to Bill and Joe. Tim, of course, was— Well, we know where Tim is. He's in the mansion. Tim is Richie's father, remember?

13

Mr. and Mrs. Willoughby continued making their way to the Melanoff mansion. Henry Willoughby was squinting and peering at street signs, complaining again about his lost bifocals, trying to see which street they were to take next; beside him, his wife was shuffling, trying not to put pressure on her blistered foot. "Are we almost there yet?" she kept asking. "I'm hungry." It reminded her husband of trips they had once taken occasionally with their children in the car, his wife in the passenger seat beside him and the four youngsters squabbling in the back seat and asking that same question over and over.

Youngsters, he mused, thinking about his own offspring. If only his four children still were! He would be nicer to them, he thought. He would not shortchange them on their allowances the way he had in the past. He would cheerfully read them bedtime stories. Occasionally, perhaps, he would take them to the zoo. They had always wanted to go to the zoo, he remembered, and he had always said no.

He thought of something, suddenly. "What was the date on the paper?" he asked his wife.

She gave a bitter laugh. "Thirty years later than we thought it was," she said. "Thirty years later than when we went off on that ridiculous vacation in the Alps."

"No, not the year. I mean what *day* is it?"

"Thursday, June seventeenth," Mrs. Willoughby told him.

"What day is Father's Day?[1] Remember Father's Day?"

"We never celebrated that, Henry. You always said it was a stupid holiday invited by greeting card manufacturers. One year the children all made you cards with their crayons and colored pencils and you told them they had wasted valuable paper and should crumple the cards and throw them away. I remember the girl cried."

"Jane," he said softly.

"Such a crybaby."

[1] In 1966 President Lyndon Johnson proclaimed the third Sunday in June as a day to honor fathers. Father's Day became a permanent national holiday when Richard Nixon signed it into law in 1972.

"I liked Jane," Mr. Willoughby said, and brushed at his eyes because they were beginning to tear up. "What day is Father's Day?"

His wife sighed. "Third Sunday in June," she told him. "So silly."

"Wasn't there a bookstore back on the last corner?" he asked.

"Yes, but we don't like books, Henry. Remember the children always wanted us to read stories to them at bedtime but we told them no? You said they should read informational material. You bought them a subscription to the *Wall Street Journal*."

"Let's go back there," he told her, "to where that bookstore was. They'll have greeting cards. I want to look at the Father's Day cards. It's not the third Sunday yet."

"Henry," his wife said, "you have it backwards. Children give cards to their father. Not the other way around."

But he had already turned and was heading back to the small store they had passed.

"And in any case," Mrs. Willoughby went on, as she hurried, with a painful limp, to keep up with him, "you just told me that they aren't children anymore. They're all grown up. Why are you—?"

But he gestured to her to shush. He was already on the front step of the small bookstore, which had, in fact, a display of books about fathers[2] in its window, along with a sign saying FATHER'S DAY: NEXT SUNDAY! So his wife followed him into the store.

"May I help you find something?" a young saleswoman asked.

But Henry Willoughby ignored her because several racks at the front of the shop were clearly marked FATHER'S DAY CARDS. He headed there.

"Not one with a dog or a cat," he muttered. "Flowers . . . maybe." He began to look through the display.

The saleswoman had remained nearby. Finally he turned to her. "I need one that isn't *to* the father, but *from* the father," he explained.

Mrs. Willoughby leaned forward. "We're about to be reunited with our children after many years," she confided.

"My goodness," the store clerk said. "Isn't that lovely? So you need a kind of *reverse* card. Let me think. Of course, we have lovely blank cards. One of those might

[2] *Fathers and Sons,* by Ivan Turgenev. *The Father Brown Mysteries* by G. K. Chesterton. And *Just Me and My Dad* by Mercer Mayer.

work, and you could write your own message. Or perhaps a card that says *thank you*?"

"What would we be thanking them for? Waiting for us? Not spending all our money?" Mrs. Willoughby asked. "Let us *hope!*"

"Do you have any that say *sorry*?" her husband asked the clerk. He was still feeling sad about Jane.

"Let me look," the clerk replied.

"Also, do you by any chance have anything edible here? I'm very hungry," his wife said. "What about a box of candy?"

The clerk looked startled. She straightened up and held her finger to her lips. "Shhhh," she said. "Not aloud."

"Not allowed? Hunger is not allowed?"

"No," said the clerk, "I meant not *aloud*. That last word you said."

"Here," said Mr. Willoughby, handing her a card with a picture of a horse on it. "This one will do. What are you talking about? My wife said 'candy.'"

"*Shhhh,*" the clerk whispered. "You know it's against the law. I wouldn't say it aloud if I were you."

"Say *candy*? Saying the word *candy*'s against the law?"

The clerk winced at the word and gestured with her

head toward the counter where the cash register was. "We used to keep it there. People get hungry when they're shopping. You-know-what was a great impulse item. We sold ever so many Milk Duds and Whoppers. But now we're trying to figure out what to offer in that space. Grapes, maybe. Or beef jerky?"

Mrs. Willoughby began to moan and wring her hands. "Milk Duds are *illegal?* Oh, Henry," she said, "we should have stayed in Switzerland!"

"Shhhh," the clerk whispered nervously. "Please don't let anyone hear you say *Oh Henry!*"[3]

[3] Oh Henry! has been a popular candy bar, with chocolate and peanuts. For a while it was so popular that whenever the major-league ballplayer Henry Rodriguez hit a home run, his fans tossed Oh Henry! bars onto the field.

14

At the same time, a few blocks away, in her little house with its freshly painted, still-gleaming blue shutters, Mrs. Poore, using her daughter Winifred's crayons, was lettering signs. B AND B, they said. She tried different designs, though she was not very good at it; there was a splotch where a crayon had broken in half midway through a letter, and the paper had torn. She drew a flower to disguise the flawed place. Then she added details, hoping to attract tourists and vacationers.

After she tacked the sign to a fence post at the end of the front walk, she sat down to wait for customers. When no one appeared after half an hour she went back, took down the sign, brought it indoors, and added another bit of information that she thought might make a difference.

"There," she said in a satisfied voice. She attached the sign once again to the fence post.

And again she went into the house. This time, feeling a little guilty because she used a fresh teabag, she made herself a cup of tea. Then she sat beside the window to wait.

15

As Mrs. Poore, sipping a cup of tea, awaited travelers in need of lodging, her two children were not at home to wait with her. Winston and Winifred had decided to go next door, to the Melanoff mansion, to apply for jobs.

They were a little nervous. Though they talked to Richie through the fence, and occasionally ventured into his yard to play, they had never been inside his magnificent home before.

"Should we knock or ring?" Winston asked his sister. They were standing together at the mansion's entrance. The huge carved door had a polished brass door knocker. But there was also a doorbell.

"Knock," said Winifred, after considering it.

"No, you," Winston told her.

Winifred gulped, then reached up and gave the door knocker a very light tap.

"Harder," Winston instructed. So his sister took a

deep breath and knocked very loudly, twice, on the door.

Eventually, as they were about to turn away and go home, the heavy door swung open. They looked up at a tall man who had a pleasant but curious look. Behind him, a wide hallway was dimly lit except for spotlights illuminating a large gold-framed portrait. They could see Richie standing in the shadows.

"Hi, Richie," Winston called.

Richie wiggled his fingers in a kind of shy wave.

"Hi, Richie," Winifred echoed, and Richie waved a second time.

"You seem to know my son," the man said. "Richie? Come up here and introduce your friends."

Richie stepped forward and stood beside his father but looked at the floor. "I don't know their names," he confessed.

"Well. Shall we remedy that?" The man looked at the pair standing on his porch and said, "Can you introduce yourselves?"

Winifred cringed, because in school they had had a lesson about how to make introductions. But now she couldn't remember if you were supposed to say "I'd like you to meet . . ." or maybe it was "It's my pleasure to introduce . . ." and in any case, she wouldn't be able to say either of those, because her cheeks had turned pink and her voice had completely disappeared. She nudged her brother.

"We're the Poore children from next door," Winston said politely.

"The poor children? Next door?" Richie's father glanced across the lawn toward the fence that separated his mansion from their little house.

"Well, yes, we are poor, but that word's a lowercase adjective. Our name has a capital P. Poore. Sometimes that happens, you know, that you have a name but it turns out also to be what you are, like how your son's name is Rich—"

Winifred poked him with her elbow, and he fell silent.

The man gave a somewhat bitter laugh. "Well," he said, "as it turns out, everything can change in an instant."

"Dad," Richie said nervously, "they're my friends."

The tall man sighed. "I'm delighted to meet you, Poores. I once knew a woman whose last name was Weaver," he said. "And guess what? She was—"

"A weaver!" Winifred said in excitement, forgetting how shy and blushy she had been.

"Actually, no," the man said. "She was a potter. But she *could* have been a weaver, couldn't she?"

His son stepped forward eagerly. "Or what if your name was Rider? And you actually were a rider? Like a champion with a bicycle? I have a bike! I have a Shimano Ultegra 6800 twenty-two-speed fully outfitted with Vuelta XRP pro wheel set!"

His father put his arm around the boy and said, "Shhhh." Then he turned to the Poore children and explained, "Richie gets overly excited."

"And sad!" Richie interrupted, his shoulders slumping. "I get overly sad sometimes, Dad! Because I don't have anyone to ride my bike with." He sighed, then added in a low voice, "It has wind-cutting aero-bladed spokes and precision bearings."

Winston took a deep breath. "Actually, sir," he said, "that's the reason my sister and I stopped by. We're poor, as I explained, and—"

Winifred took over. "And our father is in Alaska, selling encyclopedias—at least we *hope* he's selling them because we need the money—and also he might be looking for gold in his spare time. But we don't know when he'll be back, because he has problems with melancholy and—what is the other thing, Winston?"

"Occasional inebriation," Winston whispered.

"Oh, yes. He's very kind, though. We miss him very much." She paused. "Sorry. I was almost Marming," she mumbled.

Richie's father looked puzzled. "Are you trying to sell something? I think we've already bought some Girl Scout cookies, and money is increasingly tight, but I suppose we could always use another box or two."

"No sir," Winston said. "We're looking for a job."

"Like babysitting," Winifred explained. "Of course, Richie isn't a baby. But we could be, like, companions to Richie, maybe?"

"Because he's lonely," Winston added.

Richie's father seemed startled. He looked down at his son. "Is that true, Richie?" he asked. "Are you lonely? I know that on your last birthday we gave you a— What is it called?"

"International research robot," Richie replied. "It has a lightweight, precision-machined aluminum composite frame and injection-molded plastic covering that provides a strong exoskeleton."

"And doesn't it provide companionship?" his father asked.

"Well," Richie said, "its surface-mounted tactile sensors respond to touches like a pat on the head. And the points of articulation in its limbs are so precise that it can pick up and hold objects with its hands." He sighed, then added, "But no, Dad, it isn't a very good companion."

He stood beside his father with his head down. Then he whispered, "Yes, I am lonely."

The tall man stroked the top of his son's head briefly. Then he looked at the Poore children. "Why don't you come inside?" he suggested. "I think we might be able to work something out, though if you're hoping for a high salary, I'm afraid—"

His voice trailed away as he glanced outside. Then he held the door while they entered the high-ceilinged elaborate hallway, ushering them in graciously, but his attention was still on something outside. The Poore children waited with Richie beside the long, carpeted staircase that curved upward on the right. They heard Richie's father call from the front door to someone, "May I help you with something? Are you lost?" Apparently, though, the answer was no. He shrugged, closed the door, and turned his attention to the children.

He led them past the staircase and down the wide hall. Briefly he paused in front of the illuminated portrait. "My adoptive mother," he murmured, indicating the portrait of a stern-faced woman wearing oven mitts. "Nanny," he said reverently.

"I was adopted by Nanny and Commander Melanoff," he explained to the Poore children, "after I lost my biological parents when I was twelve."

"Lost?" asked Winifred. "You mean you forgot where you put them?"

"No, no," he said. "It was a tragic accident in the Alps."

He nodded reverently again to the oil-painted face, then turned away from the portrait and began to lead the children toward the drawing room.

Richie whispered an explanation to the Poores. "They wouldn't listen to any instructions," he explained, "and they wore shorts and sandals and they bought climbing equipment but they used it wrong, they put the crampons on their heads, and then they got frozen solid. My dad took me to see them once, though a telescope. We had to wait in line. And afterward we had hot chocolate."

He turned toward his father. "Didn't we, Dad? Remember, we had hot chocolate?"

"What?" Richie's father had opened the door to the drawing room. "Sorry, son," he said. "I'm afraid I wasn't paying attention. I was distracted because before I closed the front door I noticed a bizarre-looking couple approaching the front of the little house next door." He turned to Winifred and Winston. "I believe you said that's your house?"

"Yes," Winifred replied. "It's very small, but my brother just repainted the shutters."

"I could see that. Bright blue! Well, they were approaching your house. The woman was limping, and they were both wearing unattractive brown clothing. The man seemed angry about something. Any idea who they could be? Were you expecting visitors?"

Winston and Winifred both shook their heads.

"They seemed oddly familiar, as if I might have known them once."

Again, Winston and Winifred shook their heads.

"Well, I'll put it out of my mind. Nothing to do with me!" He and his son entered the elegant room and gestured that Winston and Winifred should follow. They looked around in awe at the large paintings on the walls, the thick velvet draperies, the gleaming grand piano, and the Persian rug with its muted colors.

Richie's father gestured toward a painting. "Early Holbein,"[1] he explained. "I'm going to have to sell it."

[1] Hans Holbein the Younger, a sixteenth-century German painter. He is called the Younger because—surprise!—there was also a Hans Holbein the Elder.

He looked troubled for a moment. Then he said, "Oh! I'm so sorry!" he said. "I can't stop thinking about that strange couple. I never actually introduced myself! I'm Richie's father. I guess you already know that. My name is Tim Willoughby. My siblings and I decided to keep our original last name after we were adopted, because it was all we had left of our parents. And also it was the name on the bank accounts." He held out his hand and the Poores shook it solemnly, one after the other.

"Win-Win," the Poore children murmured as a further introduction to themselves, but also because they felt as if perhaps, in an odd way, it might describe their current situation.

16

I should have looked harder for my glasses! I bet anything they were right there in the snow!" Mr. Willoughby said in a cross voice. He had leaned forward and was squinting at the sign on the fence post. "Can you read this, Frances? And by the way, you look like a flamingo,[1] standing that way."

His wife was teetering on one foot because she was holding the blistered one up to relieve the pain. "Some people think flamingos are lovely," she muttered, and hopped closer in order to read the sign.

"It says, in large letters, 'B-and-B,'" she told him. "I don't know what that means."

"Beer and bratwurst? I suppose it could be some kind of tavern," Henry Willoughby suggested.

[1] Flamingos typically stand on one leg, with the other leg tucked up. There are various theories about why they do this. But the truth is, scientists simply don't know. (Maybe they have a blister on the other foot, like Mrs. Willoughby? Ha ha.)

"No, there's no parking lot. A tavern would have a parking lot."

"Read the small print, would you? Darn, I wish I had my glasses."

His wife leaned forward. "It says Bed," she told him.

"Bed and—? B and B? What's the other B?"

"Toilet. That's all it says."

"Well, that's pretty stupid," said Henry Willoughby. "Why didn't they just say bathroom if they mean bathroom? But okay. Bed and bathroom. Right now that's sounds pretty appealing. I need to go to the bathroom, actually."

"Shall we ring the doorbell? The sign says that it usually works."

Her husband didn't reply. He was already striding toward the door of the little house. Back by the fence, Frances Willoughby tried to squeeze her swollen foot back into the shoe, which she had slipped off. Finally, she gave up and walked in a lopsided way, carrying the shoe, to join him. Before he pressed the doorbell, he said to her in a low voice, "If they ask for our name, I'm going to use a pseudonym. We don't know who runs this place."

His wife nodded, and he rang the bell.

Inside, Mrs. Poore had been watching through the

window. She had dampened a corner of her apron and wiped a small place clean on the smudged glass. Now she peered through it and examined the couple who stood at the front door. It made her nervous, running a B-and-B. What if criminals wanted a room to use as a hideout? Or . . . Goodness, she could hardly bear to think about the terrible people who might appear on her doorstep. Vegans? Hippies? Politicians?

Be strong, she told herself. *And kind. Be like Marmee.*

This couple looked ordinary, she decided. Boring, even. Brown clothes, grumpy faces, bad hairdos. She decided to open the door.

"Good afternoon." The man who stood there greeted her in a gruff, belligerent voice. "I certainly hope that the second B stands for *bathroom.*"

"Second B?" Mrs. Poore was confused.

"Where is it? The bathroom?"

She stood aside to let him in, pointed toward the bathroom, and watched in confusion as he disappeared into it.

"Sorry," the woman who had been left standing in the doorway said. "He's even worse when he has to go in the middle of the night. You know how men are."

"No," Mrs. Poore said sadly, "I suppose that once I did know how men are, but my dear husband has been gone a very long time, looking for people who would like to buy outdated encyclopedias. I believe he is in Alaska now. And he hasn't been able to send us any money. That's why we are destitute and I have opened a B-and-B."

"Actually," Mrs. Willoughby said, "I am hoping that the second B might stand for Band-Aid. I need one for my foot."

"Please come in," said Mrs. Poore. Mrs. Willoughby, still holding her shoe, hopped inside, thinking briefly that if her husband had not disappeared into the bathroom, he would probably comment that she resembled a kangaroo. She followed Mrs. Poore into the kitchen and began to lower herself into a chair.

"Stop!" Mrs. Poore said loudly. "Here, take this other chair. That one has a very wobbly leg and sometimes flings people onto the floor."

Mrs. Willoughby sat carefully in the second chair, which was itself a little wobbly since the legs seemed to be different heights. But she arranged herself with care and finally relaxed. It felt very good not to be walking anymore, even though—she looked around—she seemed to be in a very sweet but somewhat shabby place. A crayoned drawing taped to the wall was the only decoration.

Mrs. Poore was rummaging in a drawer. "Aha!" she said after a moment. "Band-Aid!" She picked it up, approached Mrs. Willoughby, and said, "Show me the hurty place."

Mrs. Willoughby pointed to her blister and winced a little as Mrs. Poore meticulously arranged the small Band-Aid over it and pressed it into place.

"I hope it sticks," Mrs. Poore murmured. "It's been used once already."

"Used?"

"We can't afford new Band-Aids every time. Thrift is an important virtue." Mrs. Poore smiled sweetly. "I always tell my children that. They accuse me of Marming, but I do think it's true, that one should always be thrifty, even with Band-Aids."

Mrs. Willoughby had not yet thought of a reply to that when her husband appeared in the kitchen. "Bed and bathroom," he announced. "Thank goodness. Now, where's the bed? I need a nap."

"I'll show you in a minute," Mrs. Poore said. "But this is a business and I must do things in a businesslike way. First, I must take your name, and you must pay me twenty-five dollars." She found a pencil stub in the same drawer where the Band-Aid had been. Then she took a crumpled paper napkin from the wastebasket and smoothed it with her hand. "Name first," she said.

"We are Mr. and Mrs., ah, Henry Frances."

Mrs. Poore wrote that on the napkin. "This will be your bill," she explained. "How many nights will you be staying?"

"Just one, I think. We're looking for relatives who live on this street. Do you happen to know anyone named Willoughby? Someone who lives in a mansion? There seems to be a mansion next door."

"Yes, indeed," Mrs. Poore said. "It has thirty-seven windows. A billionaire lives there but I'm afraid I don't know his name. He has never invited me over. Of course, I wouldn't have anything to wear if he did. I have only this one threadbare dress."

Frances Willoughby spoke up. "I know exactly how that feels! They gave us used clothing to wear when we left Switzerland. This hideous brown dress! The indignity of it!"

Mrs. Poore looked up. "You don't mean to say that you are also poor?"

"No, of course we're not!" Henry Willoughby replied.

"We have been temporarily without funds for very

complicated reasons," his wife explained. "As soon as we find our offspring . . . our heirs . . . our— Oh, I don't know what to call them!"

"Call them Tim," her husband said in a choked voice. "And Barnaby A, and Barnaby B, and— Oh dear," he snuffled, and then pulled himself together. "Jane."

"Just a moment. Are you going to be able to pay this bill?" Mrs. Poore held up the torn napkin on which she'd been writing. "Because I'm so very sorry, but I'm afraid I can't show you to your room until it's paid for in full." Secretly she'd been delighted that they had mistaken the second B for *bathroom* because it meant, she realized, they would not be expecting—or realizing they were entitled to—breakfast. She could save the handful of raisins she had been intending to add to the next morning's gruel.

"Oh, we'll pay it," Mr. Willoughby grumbled. "The American embassy finally agreed to give me dollars for my Swiss francs, even though they were soggy and stained. I think they did it to get rid of me."

"I kept mine," Mrs. Willoughby said, patting her sodden purse. "I still have them. But they're covered with mold."

"You've always been a pack rat," her husband commented. He turned to Mrs. Poore, took his wallet from his pocket, and removed some bills. "Here. You said twenty-five dollars?"

"Actually, it's twenty-six," Mrs. Poore said, and handed him the bill she had created.

"An extra dollar for *emergency medical services*?" he said, reading what she had written.

"Your wife's foot."

"My wife's *what?*"

"I have a very serious blister, Henry," Mrs. Willoughby reminded him. She was standing now and holding one leg bent, with her foot up.

"Did I mention that you look like a flamingo?" Mr. Willoughby muttered. Then, scowling, he counted out the money. "By the way," he told Mrs. Poore, "there are no towels in that bathroom. We'll need towels."

"Oh. Wait a minute." She took the bill from him and added something to it.

"Twenty-eight dollars now," she said. "Because of towels."

Mr. Willoughby's face turned deep pink. His wife recognized that as a sign that he was about to bellow. "Henry," she directed him in a terse voice, "just pay it."

He flung the money onto the kitchen table and then followed his wife to the nearby bedroom. Mrs. Poore called after them. "Toilet paper's free!" she said, graciously.

When they had closed the door behind them, she sighed an enormous sigh. She felt proud of herself. She had behaved like a businessperson instead of a pitiful, destitute Marmee of a woman. And they seemed like decent people. She wished that she had been able to put chocolates on their pillows. Ah, but the days of chocolates were gone. Chocolates were a felony now.

17

Winston and Winifred had hoped that Richie's parents would invite them to stay for dinner, but it hadn't happened. His mother had come briefly into the drawing room and had introduced herself, but then she went away again. After a while, Richie took them up the grand staircase and showed them his room, which in addition to a large bed was filled with chairs and couches and clothing, and had an adjoining playroom, where they gasped at the array of toys. But Richie yawned as he pointed to this or that and described the games and devices.

"We could come and play each day, Richie," Winston said.

"Okay." Richie glanced around the room. "But what would we play? I'm bored with everything."

"Parcheesi or something. We should talk about it, maybe over dinner," Winifred suggested. "I'm a little hungry."

Richie brightened. "Oh," he said, "that's a good idea. Shall I come over to your house?"

"Not today," Winston said. "We'll invite you for dinner another time. Your dad said he saw someone going into our house. So I suppose our mother has company."

"Yes," Winifred added. "Probably Mother would appreciate it if we stayed out of the way. I wonder where we might go to have dinner." She glanced slyly at Richie, who was examining the instruction booklet that had come with a game that was only partially unwrapped.

"This looks boring," Richie said.

"It's getting very close to dinnertime," Winston said in a loud voice. "Probably a good idea to put that away, now, Richie, and think about eating. I wonder what your family might be having for dinner."

"Boring steak, probably," Richie said.

Winston and Winifred both fell silent. Steak? They had heard of steak but had never tasted it. Dinner at their house was usually a grayish stew. Their mother had instructed them never to ask what was in it. Once, when their cat, Radish, had been missing overnight, Winston had stared at the lump of something on his spoon and murmured in dismay, *"Radish?"* But his mother had looked horrified, and replied, "Of course not. Turnip." And shortly thereafter, Radish had reappeared, wandering in through an open door, and had vomited a small mound of grass and bird feathers on the kitchen floor. The stain was still there.

"Do you have dessert at your house?" Winfred asked, after a moment.

"Yeah," Richie said with a shrug. "Boring cake, usually. Or pie."

Winfred and Winston both whimpered slightly. They waited. But Richie still did not invite them to dinner.

Finally Winifred said with a sigh, "Well, we'd better go. We'll see you tomorrow, Richie. Your dad said we should come for a few hours every day."

"Okay," Richie said. He turned away and began, with a bored look, to finish opening the package containing the new game. Then he paused suddenly and said, "Wait! What's that?"

He was looking with interest at the small object that Winston had removed from his pocket. Winston looked down at it and explained, in embarrassment, "It's just a dumb broken car. I'm going to throw it away when I get home."

"Can I see it?" Richie asked.

Winston handed him the battered toy. "My dad made it, and he gave it to me a long time ago," he explained, "but then he went away, and we don't know where he is, possibly Alaska, and the toy car broke, and he's not around, so . . ."

Riche examined it and spun its three wheels with his finger, one after another. "It just needs another wheel," he said.

"I know. Like I said, I'm going to throw it awa—"

"You think we could make one, maybe?" Richie asked. He looked excited by the idea. "A new wheel?"

Winston frowned. "Well, yeah, if we had the right tools, I suppose we—"

"We've got tools!" Richie said. "My dad has a whole set of tools from the Sharper Image catalog! And we've never used them!"

"What's the Sharper Image catalog?" Winifred whispered to her brother. Winston shrugged and whispered back, "I have no idea."

Richie, more animated than they had ever seen him, had run from his room and was calling loudly down the long staircase. "Dad? Mom? Can my friends stay for dinner?"

18

Back at the little house next door, Mrs. Poore, on hearing that her children were dining out, offered, for a small additional fee, their share of mystery meat stew to her B-and-B guests. She didn't call it that, of course. Instead, she said, "Would you care to dine with me? I have a nice beef bourguignon." Long ago, Mrs. Poore had taken French in high school. They had had a unit on cooking and dining, and she still remembered things like *coq au vin* and *beef bourguignon*. She no longer knew exactly what they were.[1] But she pronounced them correctly.

It was the first time she had ever had guests, but she knew how to be fancy. In the trash bin she found a glass jar that had held the boiled onions that she had added to the stew. Now she rinsed the smell of onions out of it, filled it with water, and went outdoors to pick flow-

[1] They are, actually, chicken cooked with wine, and beef cooked with wine. French people like to cook that way.

ers for a centerpiece. The rhododendrons belonged to her neighbors, but she could reach them through the fence to snip off some blossoms. And lily of the valley grew in a thick patch on the corner, under a stop sign; it was easy to pick a handful of that.

But when she began to arrange the flowers in the glass jar, they didn't fit. There were too many. No problem. She arranged the blossoms—crimson and white, a lovely combination, Mrs. Poore thought—and set the bulky leaves aside. *Hmm,* she thought, looking at them: *green.* Wasn't there a rule someplace, something about food groups, a rule that said people should eat green stuff? She decided to use the leaves to make a salad.

Next door, in the mansion, Richie's father, Tim Willoughby, looked at the sumptuous meal in the mansion's dining room and almost wept. He was overwhelmed with the awareness that all of this luxury would soon disappear. (At this very moment, his company's trucks were all heading from various corners of the country to the huge dump in the desert which had been designated the Candy Conflagration Area. Fires were already burning there, and the surrounding air smelled like butterscotch and mint and caramel.) Sadly he smiled at his two young guests and ushered them into the dining room, where a platter of roast beef was resting on the mahogany table. Linen napkins, rolled into napkin rings, were waiting at each place. Candles in silver candlesticks flickered. Richie's mother, using a silver spoon and fork, was tossing a salad heaped with leaves of radicchio and romaine in a handsome wooden bowl.

At the same moment, in the little kitchen next door, Mrs. Poore removed some squeezed lemon slices, left over from her lunchtime almost-tea, from the garbage. She squeezed them one more time, coaxing out a few last drops of lemon juice, and then stirred a little olive oil into the lemon juice with a bent fork. She poured the mixture over the rhododendron and lily of the valley leaves in a cracked, stained bowl, creating a salad that she planned to serve to Henry and Frances Willoughby.

The salad was a very unfortunate decision. She should have paid better attention in her high school botany class. She didn't know, hadn't learned, didn't remember, that both plants[2] were highly poisonous.

[2] The first written account of rhododendrons goes back to the fourth century BC in Greece, when ten thousand soldiers were poisoned by honey of *Rhododendron luteum*. And lily of the valley? It contains about twenty poisonous glycosides, including convalatoxin, convalarin, convalamarin, and saponins.

19

In their room (actually, Mrs. Poore's bedroom, but they didn't know that, of course), Mr. and Mrs. Willoughby discussed their situation and made plans. Glancing through the one small window (one of the six windows in the little house, as Winifred had noted many times), Henry Willoughby said, suddenly, "That must be it."

"*What* must be it?" his wife asked.

"What're you, a parrot? You always repeat what I say."

She glared at him. *"Squawk,"* she said, parrot-like.

He ignored that. "I meant that the house next door—that mansion—is probably the one where the person named Willoughby lives. Remember what that kid at our old house said? Someone named Willoughby lives in a mansion? On this street? This is the only mansion around. It has to be it."

"Let's go ring the doorbell and find out," his wife

suggested. "I'm going in my socks, though. I'm never putting on those shoes again."

Her husband frowned. "I'm hungry. And that woman? The one who overcharged us for the room? She said she'd give us dinner. Well, *give*'s the wrong word. She's charging us for it. Probably overcharging. But let's eat, get some sleep, and then ring the mansion's doorbell tomorrow."

That made sense, his wife thought. She was very hungry as well. They were actually glad that Mrs. Poore had invited them; they had no idea where to find a restaurant—the whole neighborhood had changed so much since they had left it thirty years earlier—and in any case they didn't relish another long walk. But they felt a little disheveled. Mrs. Willoughby had put on a pair of thick socks and was shuffling about in them because she couldn't bear the thought of squeezing her sore feet back into the too-small high heels that had produced blisters. Her husband had a very stubbly face because there was no hot water in the bathroom and he couldn't shave, even though the embassy in Switzerland had provided them with basic toiletries: toothbrushes, combs, and a razor.

"Am I remembering correctly," Frances Willoughby asked Henry Willoughby with a sigh, "that we were once somewhat, ah, elegant?"

He looked up from his efforts. He was trying to rub off the spots that had accumulated on his shirt: coffee and toothpaste and something else that he couldn't identify. "I was," he replied. "I don't remember that you ever were."

Mrs. Willoughby winced. "I had that nice dress that I wore on holidays," she reminded him.

"It had those swirly things on it," her husband said, "and some feather decorations. It made you look like a peacock."

She pouted. *"Sticks and stones may break my bones,"* she chanted, but he wasn't listening. "And by the way: You need a haircut. And a shave. You're very stubbly and unkempt. It makes you look old."

Mr. Willoughby looked at his wife with an irritated frown. "You had to mention that, didn't you?"

"Mention what?"

"Our ages. I was hoping to forget about this odd problem."

She remembered then. "We're actually very young!" she said. "Younger than everyone we knew before we went to Switzerland! And—ha ha!—they're old now."

"Yes, but our children—"

"I'm not going to think about them," Mrs. Willoughby said.

"But they—" her husband began.

But Mrs. Willoughby put her hands over her ears and chanted loudly, *"La la la."*

Mr. Willoughby gave up on the conversation about the children, though he was now remembering them with great fondness. Little Jane had had such a winsome smile. And the eldest—Tim—he was a stalwart boy, a natural leader who had often spoken on behalf of all four of them when they wanted something: a meal, perhaps; clean pajamas; or fresh water in the bathtub. And the twins! It hadn't been fair, he now thought, to make them share a name, and just one sweater. They deserved *two*. Oh, what bad parents he and his wife had been! He dabbed his eyes.

"Well," he said, pulling himself together after a moment, "let's go to dinner. Maybe there will be candlelight so no one will notice how we look."

When they arrived for dinner in the Poore kitchen, though, there were no candles. Light came from the dim bulb that hung, swaying, from the ceiling. Against the wall, a refrigerator with rust around the door handle made an agonized wheezing sound. Plates of varying sizes were arranged at three places. A large bowl of salad was in the center of the table, and the stew bubbled in its pot on the stove.

"If I could just afford a microwave, I could've heated that stew up so much faster," Mrs. Poore commented. "It's one of the things we'll buy, when my Ben comes home with his fortune."

"What's a microwave?" Mrs. Willoughby whispered to her husband.

But he didn't know. He shrugged and muttered in reply, "Some newfangled gizmo." They both watched as their hostess poked at the stew with a long-handled spoon. It didn't look very appetizing. But they were hungry.

"How about if I go ahead and serve this salad?" Mr. Willoughby said, and reached to the center of the table, where the bowl of greens waited.

20

Winifred and Winston Poore, at the same moment, were marveling at their dinner. Several courses! Soup, to start with. Back in their house, soup was a frequent meal, but it was always the main course, and consisted of the previous night's stew with water added. But here, in the mansion where Richie lived with his parents, the first course, served by a maid, was a delicious thick soup in porcelain bowls with a thin gold rim. And special soup spoons! The Poore children had to watch carefully to see what utensil to use, because there were several pieces of silverware lined up at each place.

"Yum!" Winslow said, after his first spoonful.

"Wild mushroom bisque," Richie's mother explained.

"You could kill someone with wild mushrooms if you picked the wrong kind," Richie announced. "That's how the King of the Elephants died, in *Babar.* He ate a toxic shiitake."

Then he added, "I have the whole set of Babar

books. First editions. After dinner I'll show you my Book Room."

"What about these mushrooms?" Winifred asked. She suddenly felt a little nervous even though the soup was delicious.

"No need to worry," Ruth Willoughby reassured her. "These are quite safe. Actually, Tim and I have studied mushrooms[1] quite extensively. The ones in your soup are morels and chanterelles."

"I wish I could study something interesting, like mushrooms," Winifred said. She finished eating her soup now that she'd been reassured. "Something besides reading and arithmetic," she added.

"My sister is a very good student," Winston explained, "but she's a little bored with school."

"Choose any subject," Richie suggested, "and then come to my Book Room and I'll give you books about it. I have books about every single thing. You can take them home."

"Geology?" asked Winifred. "I'm very interested in geology."

"Done," Richie said.

[1] Mushroom experts are called *mycologists*. And the deadliest mushrooms are called *Amanita*. Do not ever taste one.

The door opened and from the kitchen the maid appeared. She moved about the table, quietly removing the empty soup bowls.

Richie's father tapped on his water glass to get everyone's attention. "Before I serve the roast beef," he said, "I'd like to make a little toast."

Richie whispered to the Poore children, "My dad loves to make toasts. Sometimes they go on forever."

"Here's to our lovely guests," Mr. Willoughby said. "Winifred and Winston! So good to have you here. Here's to your companionship with Richie!"

Winifred and Winston smiled politely and prepared to reach for their forks. The roast beef smelled delicious.

"And here's to my lovely wife!" Tim Willoughby went on. Richie's mother smiled affectionately at her husband.

"Next, to my adoptive father, Commander Melanoff, who is dining in his own suite tonight, first because of his advanced age. Ninety-seven years old!" Everyone murmured appreciatively. "And second because he is understandably devastated by the recent turn of events in the world of confectionary."

"What does that mean?" Winston whispered to Richie.

Richie shrugged. He didn't know.

"And to Other Barnaby," Tim went on, in a reverent voice. "A moment of silence in his honor."

"Is that somebody who's dead?" Winifred whispered to Richie.

"No," Richie replied. "Just silent. Shhhh."

They all sat quietly for a moment, even Winston and Winifred, though they had no idea why. (Other Barnaby, Commander Melanoff's son who, curiously, had the same name as the Willoughby twins, though his Barnaby was followed by Junior, had once been president of the family company. There had even been some discussion of a new candy to be called Junior Mints, after him. But he had decided to become a Trappist monk, instead, and now lived silently in a monastery in western Massachusetts where he was known as Brother Barnaby.)

Finally, still holding his glass up, Tim Willoughby went on. "And in memory of beloved Nanny! Such a wonderful woman, and a fantastic cook!

"And now," he went on, "I believe I'll recite one of my father's poems. *There once was a woman named Nanny*—"

His wife interrupted. "No, Tim. Not the naughty one," she said in a stern voice. "Not when we have company."

Richie, giggling, leaned toward the Poore children. "It's about her bum," he whispered.

Tim Willoughby sighed. "Well then, we'll not bother with the poem. Children? A toast from each of you, please?"

Richie held up his glass. "To my new friends!" he said.

Everyone was looking at Winifred and Winston. Finally, Winifred raised her glass and said, "To my father! May his travels end soon!"

Now only Winston was left. "Uh, to my cat, Radish!" he said, after a moment.

"You have a *cat?*" Richie said loudly. "I want a cat! Why can't I have a—"

"Time to dine," his father said. He began to serve the roast beef.

21

Next door, in the Poores' kitchen, Mrs. Willoughby put down her fork suddenly. "I don't feel well," she announced.

"You look a little ashen," her husband said. "Not a great look on you."

"Sticks and stones will—" she began. Then she interrupted herself. "Excuse me," Mrs. Willoughby said in a stricken voice, and ran to the bathroom.

"Whatever is wrong with her?" her husband said. Then he clutched his stomach, leaned over, and vomited on the cat.

Mrs. Poore, who had not eaten any salad, looked about her kitchen with dismay. Running a B-and-B was not turning out to be very much fun.

22

The doorbell rang at the Melanoff mansion shortly after dessert (strawberry shortcake! The Poore children had heard of such a thing but had never actually seen it—much less tasted it—before) had been served. The maid placed the last plate on the table and then scurried off to answer the door. But in a moment she was back.

"It's a very distressed woman," she told Richie's father in a low voice.

"Oh dear," Tim Willoughby said. "Will it ruin our dessert if you bring her in here so we can find out what she wants?"

"Sir," the maid said, "nothing ruins strawberry shortcake. I'll go and get her."

Winifred and Winston looked up in surprise when their mother appeared in the doorway, wringing her hands.

"I'm Mrs. Poore, your next-door neighbor," she said to Mr. Willoughby in an agitated voice. "I'm their mother." She pointed to her two children.

"No need to check on them," Richie's mother said. "They're behaving very nicely."

"And look, Mother—we're having strawberry shortcake!" Winifred told her.

"May I get you a plate? There's plenty." Richie's mother suggested.

"No! I mean not now! I'd love to have some another time! But right now I have an emergency! And I don't have a telephone—I'm too poor!"

Winston began to explain. "Our name is Poore, you see; but we're *also* poor. Same as Richie? His name is Richie, and—"

Winifred whispered, "Shhhh."

"*We* have a telephone," Richie announced. "We actually have many telephones. We have a Grandstream GXP state-of-the-art phone system with dual gigabit network ports. The display languages include Arabic, Chinese, Croatian, Czech, Dutch, English . . . "

"She doesn't need to know that, Richie," his father said gently.

"French, German, Hebrew, Hungarian, Italian . . ." Richie couldn't seem to stop.

"What exactly is your emergency, Mrs. Poore? Should we call 911?"

"Yes! I had these guests in my house, I mean my B-and-B, and right in the middle of dinner—"

Richie interrupted. "Japanese, Korean, Polish, Portuguese . . ."

"Those must be the people I saw from the window," Tim Willoughby said. "They looked vaguely familiar. What are their names? I think I must have met them in the past."

"Their names. Their names. Ah . . ." Mrs. Poore wrinkled the hem of her stained apron nervously in her hands. "They're Mr. and Mrs. Henry, I think. Or maybe Mr. and Mrs. Frances. I forget. One of those. Anyway, it doesn't matter, because they're both of them lying unconscious on the floor now, and my *cat!* You should see what happened to the cat!"

"Russian, Slovenian, Spanish, Turkish. And that's it." Richie looked up, beaming.

"Oh dear, is the cat all right?" his mother asked Mrs. Poore.

"I suppose so, but she'll have to have a bath, and she hates baths! She's completely covered in—"

"We have call forwarding, call hold, call transfer, call waiting, caller ID, and voice mail," Richie declared.

His father had gone to the hall and was dialing 911.

"Do sit down, Mrs. Poore. Have some strawberry shortcake," Richie's mother said in a gracious voice.

"Emergency vehicles are on their way!" Richie's father announced as he returned from the hall.

His wife served a plate of dessert to Mrs. Poore. "Whipped cream?" she offered.

"They didn't throw up in my bed, did they?" Winifred whispered in an alarmed voice to her mother.

"Everywhere," Mrs. Poore told her daughter. "Absolutely everywhere." Then she turned to Richie's mother. "Yes, whipped cream, please."

"Diarrhea?" Winston asked. "Usually when you get—"

Mrs. Poore nodded and put her head into her hands. "Yes. The whole catastrophe," she whimpered. Then she lifted her head, looked at the dessert in front of her, dipped her finger into the whipped cream, tasted it, and said, "Yum."

"I'd offer after-dinner mints," Mr. Willoughby explained to everyone at the table, "but as most of you know, mints have become . . ." He hesitated and choked back tears. "In fact, all candy has become . . . Oh dear, this is such a monumental disaster. Our fortune has depended on— And now—" He put his head in his hands.

Outside, from a distance, they heard sirens as the ambulances approached.

23

Poor Ben Poore was still trudging along in western Canada, weighed down by both his backpack and his sorrow. He missed his dear children. He regretted the four hundred and three bad decisions he had made in his life.[1]

Vaguely he thought about changing his name, maybe to Rich—but with an "e," the way Poore had an "e." *Riche.* But he realized people would pronounce it "Reesh" and he didn't like the sound of that. Also: his wife. Though her name was Patricia, she was often called Trish. That wouldn't work, for sure: Trish Rich? Or Trish Reesh?

Anyway, he thought, the name Poore had an illustrious history. One of his grandfathers had been a professor of something. And an uncle was a chiropractor.

[1] Kicking the dog in Akron, Ohio, was number 345. He kept a list. Smoking a cigarette when he was thirteen was number 106.

He too could be illustrious, he thought. If only he could sell these dratted encyclopedias. Maybe in the next town — Prince George. Surely, he thought, there were people in Prince George who yearned to be educated and informed.

Behind him on the empty road he heard the faint sound of an engine. A car or truck was approaching. He took a deep breath, adjusted the backpack, tried to assume a pleasing and non-dangerous facial expression, and held out his thumb.

24

At the hospital, teams of doctors worked on the couple who had been brought in by ambulance from the house where they had been found unconscious. They gave them IVs and steroids and antibiotics and X-rays and MRIs and EKGs and glucose and biopsies and everything else they could think of.[1] Meanwhile, in the administration office of the hospital, there was a flurry of confusion.

"This makes no sense," the hospital director said. He picked up one of the two wallets that were lying on his desk. "They both have medical insurance cards, but the insurance company says they've never heard of them."

"And I called the address on their driver's licenses," the assistant hospital administrator said. "It's a very nice house—I drive past it every day on my way to work—but the woman who answered said her name is O'Leary and her family has lived there for years. She's

[1] Do not under any circumstances try any of this at home.

never heard of— What was the name again?" She picked up one wallet, peered at the ID, and said, "Willoughby."

"There are credit cards," the secretary said. "But they've all expired years ago. I called the Mastercard number, but they thought I was nuts. And no, they won't cover the hospital bill."

The chief administrator turned to the young EMT who had driven the ambulance. "Explain again where you found them."

The EMT repeated the address. "It's a very strange little house. I wouldn't even call it a house, really—it's so tiny. The shutters are a nice freshly painted blue, and you could tell that ordinarily, when no one has been vomiting everywhere, it's very tidy. But there's a straw hat hanging on the door. And the refrigerator makes a grinding noise—*eeew, eeew, eeew*—as if it has pulmonary problems."

"And this couple lives there?"

"No, the woman who lives there, a Mrs. Poore, said they were her guests. But she didn't really know them. She wasn't even sure of their names."

"The drivers' licenses both say Willoughby."

"I know. But this Mrs. Poore? She says that the name they told her was something else. An alias, I guess."

A police officer was standing in the doorway, listening. He hadn't been paying much attention because it wasn't a homicide or a burglary—those were the things that interested him. But now he straightened his shoulders and stepped forward. "Alias?" he said. "Did someone say *alias*? That's my department!" He took a small notebook from his pocket, wrote *ALIAS* in large letters and waited, poised, for more information.

"And there's a problem," the EMT went on.

"Definitely my department," the police officer said, and began to write: *PROBLEM.*

"The thing is," the EMT explained, "according to the DOB—"

"What's that mean? DOB?" the police officer asked, his pencil waiting.

"Date of birth."

The police officer wrote that down.

The EMT continued. "According to the DOB on the licenses, they should be sixty-something. Close to seventy."

"They're not close to seventy. No way." The young doctor who had seen the couple in the emergency ward stepped forward.

"No, they're way younger," the EMT agreed. "I'd say thirties, tops."

At her desk, the secretary tapped the keys on her computer. “I’m going to Google them,” she said. “Tell me the names again.”

The administrator picked up the wallets. “Willoughby,” he said, looking at the first one. “Henry, and—” He opened the second wallet. “Some soggy money in here. Foreign, it looks like. Here’s the name: Frances.”

Everyone waited. The secretary typed in the names. After a pause, she looked up, her eyes wide. “Whoa,” she said. “I got an obituary! They’re dead! Both of them!”

“Dead?” the policeman repeated, and began writing in his notebook. “My department for sure!”

“They’re not dead! They both had pulses,” the EMT said. “I took them myself. And blood pressures.”

The secretary read from the screen. “Died in Switzerland. Mountain climbing accident.”

The assistant administrator said, “I climbed Mount Washington once,” he said. “In New Hampshire? But I was way younger then.”

“Oh, be quiet,” said his boss. “What else does it say?” He turned to his secretary.

“This is weird.” She looked up, puzzled. “That accident was thirty years ago.”

At that moment the office door opened and a white-coated man appeared. "Sorry to interrupt," he said. "But I thought you should have this information."

He handed a clipboard thick with papers to the administrator. "I'm from Pathology,"[2] he explained.

"Spell that," said the police officer, and then listened carefully to the spelling. He added *PATHOLOGY* to his notebook page.

"The thing is," the pathologist said, "we've been looking at these slides down in the path lab. They're from that couple that was biopsied in the ER."

"Henry and Frances Willoughby," the secretary said. "I just Googled them. And—"

"They were frozen."

"That's what the obituary says," the secretary, still looking at her computer screen, explained. "Frozen solid. They were inadequately dressed, and the temperature was—"

The administrator interrupted her. He turned to the pathologist. "You mean that you took the biopsied material and froze it to make slides for your microscope?"

[2] Pathology is the study of changes in tissue produced by diseases. Pathologists spend a lot of time peering into microscopes.

“No, I mean—”

“Hold it,” said the police officer. “I’m getting this down. Frozen, you say? Same as the movie? My kid loves that movie. She’s always singing—” He began to sing the words. *“Let it gooooo . . .”*

The pathologist interrupted him. “Would you shut up?” he said. “What I mean is that the cell structure indicates that the tissues themselves, long before we got the specimens, had been frozen. And then, at some later time, defrosted.”

The room fell silent.

“Would insurance cover that?” someone asked.

25

Back at the mansion, with the excitement of the emergency over, the Poore children and their mother all had a second helping of strawberry shortcake. Then Winifred and Winston went upstairs with Richie to his playroom. Richie was carrying the broken toy car.

"I wish I had a little car like this," he murmured.

"But, Richie," Winston pointed out, "you have a zillion toy cars. Battery operated, hand carved, glow in the dark, remote control, every other kind. You don't need another car. And this one isn't anything special. It's just a crummy, busted—"

"I know," Richie said, stroking the toy, "but your father made it for you."

Winifred and Winston both fell silent. They were thinking: *Your dad pays the bills for everything you order. Your dad buys you all those toys.* But they knew that it wasn't the same. It made them feel sad.

Finally, Winifred, to change the subject, said, "Could I see your Book Room, Richie?"

Richie put the little broken car carefully on a shelf in his playroom and then opened a door to reveal what looked like a private library. There were shelves crowded with books against every wall.

"It's alphabetically arranged by category," Richie explained. "My dad hired a librarian to come in and do it. You see, over here? By the window? Nonfiction: Aeronautics and Animals and Architecture."

He showed them around the room, pointing out the labels for different categories.

"What if you just want to read a story?" Winston asked. "I like stories."

"Over here, on the north wall. All fiction. Of course, you have your choice of fantasy, historical fiction, adventure, realism, humor, or—"

"Why do some books have MBD written on them?" Winifred asked.

Richie thought for a moment. "I forget. No, wait —now I remember. MBD means Might Be Distressing. I'm supposed to ask my mother before I read one of those."

"Why is this one MBD?" Winston had reached for a book in the beginning of the nonfiction section. She handed it to Richie.

"It's about mountain climbing," Richie said.

"So? Why would that be distressing? Over there in the S department is a book about skydiving, but it isn't MBD. I think skydiving is scarier than mountain climbing.

"And here!" Winifred chimed in. "In the Gs! A book about grizzly bears, but it's not MBD. But in the O section: a book about orphans—and it's MBD. I feel quite certain that orphans are not as distressing as grizzly bears. I'm not distressed at all about orphans, not one bit. Why would *orphans* be MBD?"

Richie shrugged. "I don't know. I never thought about it."

"It's a mystery, then. I like mysteries," Winston said. "Let's try to solve it!"

"How?" Winifred and Richie laughed at themselves, because they had said "How?" in unison.

"Well," Winston suggested, "we'll start by making a stack of all the MBD books, and then we'll see what they have in common."

"Yes!" Winifred said, and she started the stack immediately by placing *Orphans* on top of *Mountain Climbing* on the table in the center of the room. Then she reached for another book with the curious marking. "Hmm," she said, examining it. "*Parenting*." She added it to the small stack and reached for the next.

26

Mrs. Poore went home after dessert, carrying a container of leftovers her hosts had kindly offered her. The two mysterious unconscious B-and-B guests were gone, carried away in two ambulances, but a terrible mess had been left behind. Even Radish, the cat, who usually liked messes and frequently created some of his own, had fled.

She had suggested to her children that they might return with her to the house and help with the cleaning. Maybe, she had said, even Richie would like to join them? They could all work together? But the children had been unenthusiastic.

"I prefer not to. I don't know how to clean things up," Richie had said politely. "I never had to learn. We have maids."

"I think we should stay here," Winston had told her. "We've been hired to be companions to Richie."

"Yes, we're getting *paid!*" Winifred added. "And anyway, Mother, I'm afraid I might get sick if I have to clean up somebody's else's sickness. I'm quite certain it's better if you do it alone."

"Well," Mrs. Poore replied, "you sure you're getting paid?"

The children nodded. "Lots," Winston said, though he wasn't certain if it was true. Actually, Mr. Willoughby had just told him, quite mournfully, that money was soon going to be in short supply.

"In that case you should stay, I guess," their mother decided. "But not too late. I want you home by . . ." She hesitated. "Are you being paid by the hour?" she asked.

"Yes," Winston fibbed. "Absolutely."

"Well, then, stay. But not past midnight. Unless, of course, he agrees to a higher rate after midnight. In that case, I think you could even work all night.

"But don't expect me to save any of these leftovers for you," she added, carefully stacking the containers of roast beef and strawberry shortcake so that she could carry them home. "There's leftover salad you can have if you're hungry later. The guests barely finished theirs before they fainted."

Now, back in her kitchen, she looked around with a sigh, then set the leftovers on the counter beside the squealing refrigerator. She put on her apron, filled a pail with water from the sink, picked up her mop, and began to clean.

27

Back at the Book Room, the three children continued their examination of the shelves.

"Just point me to the geology books, okay?" Winifred said. "I am so interested in geology, and I'm hoping to—"

"Here's another MBD!" Winston announced. He added it to the pile of books that were marked with the identifying letters.

"And one more," said Richie, who had found one on a low shelf near the corner.

"I just don't get it," Winston said, finally, looking at the stack. "Are you sure that what's it stands for, Richie? Might Be Distressing? He picked up the book he had just added and read the title: "*Cryogenics*. Huh?"

Winifred laughed. "I bet that one means Most Boringly Dull."

But Richie was certain. "No, for sure it's Might Be Distressing. I remember when it started. When my parents first created the Book Room—it used to be a nursery, when I was little; it had a rocking horse and a big teddy bear—they sent away to a bookstore and a truck came, filled with books. My mother was arranging them, but she kept coming across things that she said might upset me. She was going to throw them away, but my dad said no, he'd paid a lot for them, so keep them but just put special markings on them. Might Be Distressing. And they told me maybe I could read them when I was grown."

"Look! Here's one called *The Swiss Postal System,*" Winston announced, choosing another from the stack. "Why would that be distressing? Who would even care about that? Can you think of one single person who is interested in the Swiss postal system?"

"Nope," his sister said.

"No," Richie replied.

"I am, in a way," a deep voice said, "but we will not discuss it further."

The door had opened and a man was standing there, leaning on a cane. His hair was white, and he was wearing a bathrobe. "You are looking at a ruined man," he announced.

"Oh! My goodness! Good evening, Grandfather!" Richie said in a startled voice.

28

Back in the emergency ward, Mr. Willoughby finally opened his eyes. He turned his head and looked at his wife, who was lying on a nearby stretcher.

"Your hair's a mess," he murmured to her. "You look like a shih tzu."

She turned her own head, weakly, and stared at him. *"Sticks and stones may break my bones,"* she chanted, and then fell silent because she had no energy and couldn't remember what came next.

A nearby nurse hastened to reassure her. "No, dear, you have no broken bones! You have severe gastroenteritis and potentially fatal ventricular tachycardia."

A doctor who was rearranging some instruments on a tray looked up and added, "The lab found thirty-eight different cardiac glycosides in your cells. The general structure of a cardiac glycoside consists of a steroid molecule, the nucleus of which consists of four fused rings to which other functional groups such as methyl, hydroxyl, and aldehyde groups can be attached to influence the overall molecule's biological activity."

Mr. Willoughby raised his head slightly on his stretcher and muttered, "I hate when people don't speak English."

"Lie back, dear," the nurse told him. "You don't want to dislodge your sphygmomanometer."[1]

The doctor continued: "The lab also found grayanotoxins, which are low-molecular-weight hydrophobic compounds structurally characterized as polyhydroxylated cyclic diterpenes."

Mr. Willoughby groaned. "Don't listen to them, Frances," he said to his wife. "They aren't speaking English. We're in some weird foreign country. Even Switzerland was better."

"You can Google all of this when you get home," the doctor remarked.

"We can *what? Google*? Is that what you said? Did you mean *gargle*?"

[1] Blood pressure cuff. Don't you love learning new words?

The doctor ignored him and said, "Also, it appears that you have both been frozen and then thawed."

"Well, we *knew* that, you big showoff!" Frances Willoughby said in a very irritated voice, and reached down under the sheet to rub her blistered foot.

29

Winston and Winifred called, "See you tomorrow, Richie!" and returned next door to their house for the night. Radish, the cat, leapt out of the weeds and scurried inside behind them when they opened the door. They found their mother at the kitchen table, enjoying the last of the leftover shortcake while in the corner her mop soaked in a bucket of gray water. Radish sniffed at it but turned away in disgust.

"Are the guests all right?" Winston asked.

Mrs. Poore shrugged. "I haven't heard. I'm going to charge them extra for the cleanup, though. If they're alive, of course."

"Poor people."

"No, no, *we* are the poor Poore people! We don't have enough money, there's no food in the refrigerator, your father is who-knows-where, not a single person has called to make a reservation for the B-and-B, and—"

"But, Mother," Winifred began. "we have no telephone. How could anyone—"

"Oh, hush, dear. You sometimes have a whiny voice."

"I only meant—"

"It's bedtime," Mrs. Poore told the children. "Go to bed. And by the way, there are no sheets. The sheets were ruined by the, you know, sickness. The throwing-up. I think I'm going to charge them more for the laundry. Maybe another ten dollars." She reached into the wastebasket for a crumpled paper towel and began to prepare a new invoice.

"Clean sheets would be lovely for the next B-and-B guests, Mother," Winifred said, "but without a telephone, how can—"

"Didn't you hear me say *bedtime*? You just yammer on and on."

Winifred sighed. "Come on, Winston," she said to her brother. "We'd better get some sleep. We promised Richie we'd be there first thing in the morning."

As the two made their way out of the kitchen, Winston reminded his sister of something. "Actually, we also have a Book Room." He pointed to a closed door.

"That's only a storage closet," Winifred replied.

“Yes, but it’s a *big* closet. And it’s absolutely crammed with—”

“I know. Outdated encyclopedias.”

Both children groaned.

30

It was late afternoon. While the three children amused themselves upstairs in the playroom, Richie's father was in the drawing room below. Tim Willoughby did have an office at the candy factory, but he rarely went there, because the factory ran so smoothly. It was filled with huge stainless-steel machines that mixed and stirred and flavored and compressed the ingredients, sliced them into bars, then weighed and measured them. Bright-colored labels, thousands every hour, appeared from the huge label-making machine and went by conveyer to the label-pasting machine, arriving there just as the newly filled boxes of candy appeared from another direction. The labels were slapped onto each box, then went to the robot, which placed the boxes, tightly packed, into large cartons; from there the cartons moved slowly and heavily onto a loading dock to which trucks backed up. One after another, every day, trucks filled with all varieties of confections, including the best-selling Lickety Twist, left the factory and rumbled across the highways to the supermarkets and movie theaters and variety stores where they would be sold, across the United States and even Canada.

Usually Tim Willoughby sipped coffee and turned the pages of his paper to find the latest baseball scores while his trucks revved their engines every morning. There was a telephone beside him. Occasionally a call would report that a truck had had a flat tire and was slightly delayed. Sometimes there was news, relayed by telephone, of yet another accolade: "DULUTH KIDS CHOOSE FAVORITE SWEET," for example, when Minnesota children had, to no one's surprise, selected Lickety Twist. His nearby laptop showed continuous videos: a troop of Boy Scouts touring the factory, wearing surgical caps so that no single hair would ever make its way into a huge mixing bowl; a woman celebrating her one hundredth birthday in a midwestern nursing home would be interviewed, describing with a grin how she had sucked on a Lickety Twist every day of her adult life; an Employee of the Month pumped his fist in the air when he was given the news that he was entitled to a prime parking space with a special identifying sign: SWEET SPOT.

But not today. Today was one terrible bit of news after another. The stock market had plunged. Sugar refineries were reporting huge losses because of the candy ban. The CIA was reporting an upsurge in chocolate smuggling throughout Central America. Sullen teenagers had been charged with illegal possession and were pictured on the news being arraigned in juvenile court. And Hollywood was abuzz about plans for several horror films featuring death-by-candy.

Most of Consolidated Confectionaries' trucks were returning, now empty, from the desert conflagration site. The factory machinery had fallen silent. Four hundred workers had been notified that their jobs were ending.

Tim Willoughby leafed through his bank statements with mounting despair and watched his wealth disappear.

31

One of the company's large vehicles was actually heading south from Anchorage, Alaska, toward Prince George, Canada, a very long drive.

The driver had stopped overnight at a Days Inn in Whitehorse. Then he had driven all the next day and slept the second night in the cab of his truck. Now, finally, he was just beyond the small town of Smithers. Only a couple hundred miles left to go. But he was tired and bored, and needed someone to talk to, just to keep him awake. When he saw a hitchhiker on the road ahead, he eased up on the gas and put his foot on the brake, slowing the vehicle to a stop.

"Mister?" he called to the hitchhiker. "Could you use a ride all the way to Prince George?"

"Sure could," the hitchhiker said.

"That backpack looks heavy," the truck driver commented.

Ben Poore wrestled the pack from his own shoulders and lifted it up into the cab of the truck. Then he climbed up after it. “It doesn’t feel heavy when it’s filled with the knowledge of centuries,” he said to the driver. “Let me tell you about this incredible encyclopedia.”

32

"Dear?" Richie's mother appeared at the drawing room door. His father looked up.

"Yes?"

"Someone from the hospital's on the phone. About that couple who got sick next door?"

Richie's father sighed, put his disheartening bank statement down, and went to the hall where the telephone sat on an antique table with curved legs. He hoped the call wouldn't take long. He was ready to put the bad bank information aside for the time being, because he had promised his son, along with those odd children from next door, that he would open up the elaborate tool set he had once purchased, and that together they would repair the small broken toy car that for some reason seemed to have significance for Richie. It would be a distraction.

Upstairs, the two boys waited impatiently for Richie's father. They had become bored with the MBD book project, having found absolutely nothing that connected the marked books to each other. Orphans had nothing in common with a study of private railway travel. Mountain-climbing was unconnected to the Swiss postal system. And Winifred, in particular, had lost interest in anything else when she happened on a book (no MBD label) about geology, her passion; she was curled up now in a comfortable chair reading about magnetite, iron pyrite, and tetradymite.

"All right, boys, let's get started!" The door to the playroom opened and Richie's dad appeared, carrying a heavy box. "Look: I've got my eighty-nine-piece general purpose tool kit, never opened!

"Excuse me, I meant 'Boys and girl!'" he added, remembering Winifred.

She looked up. "It's okay," she told him. "I'm just going to sit here reading."

"All right. Let us know if you decide to join us. I'm sorry to keep you waiting, boys. I had to take an odd telephone call."

He set the box on the playroom floor and the two boys sprawled beside it and tugged it open.

"Why was your phone call odd?" Winifred asked. "I'm always interested in odd." She marked her page in the geology book and set it aside.

Tim Willoughby had picked up the small broken car

and was examining it. "We may have to order a new wheel for this," he said. "I doubt if my toolbox contains wheels." He looked over at Winifred. "Ah, odd because—"

"Cool!" Winston exclaimed, leaning over the large now open box. "Eighteen different wrenches!"

"Six screwdrivers!" Richie added, holding up two of them. "All sizes!"

"Richie," his father said, "turn on your computer and see if you can find out how to order wheels, okay? Nothing expensive. Sorry," he said to Winifred. "I got distracted. The phone call was from the director of the hospital," he told her.

"Is that odd?"

"No, it's not. I donate a lot of money to the hospital. I mean, I used to." He frowned for a moment. "I suppose those days are over now."

"We're ruined," Richie whispered to his friends, although he still didn't understand exactly what that meant.

"Of course the hospital people don't know yet about my changed circumstances. So the director calls me often, wanting to know if I'd like a lab named for me, or maybe a room, or a whole ward. They already have the Richie Willoughby Fracture Unit. I donated that after my son broke his ankle. We were skiing and he hadn't paid adequate attention to the instructor; he missed a turn on the intermediate slope."

"It wasn't my fault, Dad! It was my dumb boots!" Richie looked over from where he was now seated at his computer.

"Richie, those boots were the best. Thin-shell construction and an eighteen-millimeter oversize pivot. And they were perfect with your skis!"

"But I didn't want skis! I wanted a snowboard!"

His father turned back to Winifred. "And there's also the Commander Melanoff Orphan Care Department. I funded that some years ago and named it after my dad."

"*Orphan* care?" Winifred sat up straight. She and Winston glanced meaningfully at each other. A book about orphans was in the stack they had created in the Book Room.

"My wife was an orphan. So, in fact, was I. We have a particular concern for orphans. But back to the phone call and why it was odd . . ."

"Look! There's a high-tension hacksaw!" Winston was still rummaging in the huge toolbox.

Richie was now scrolling through sources of toy

car wheels on his computer. "Winston, measure the wheels and see what size we need," he said.

"You remember the couple who needed the emergency care last night?" his father continued, talking to Winifred. "You were here when your mother came over and we called 911."

Winifred nodded. "Of course. That's why I didn't have sheets on my bed last night. They threw up on my sheets before they fainted."

"Well, they're out of the intensive care unit. And they'll be discharged from the hospital in a couple of days. But no one could reach your mother—"

"We can't afford a telephone," Winifred said with a sad look.

"And they don't seem to have a home," Richie's father went on, "or any money."

"They paid my mom in advance," Winston said, looking up from the toolbox. "I think they paid her twenty-eight dollars."

"Well, that seems to be all they had, except for a fairly large amount of damp, wadded-up Swiss francs in the woman's purse."

"So that's why the phone call was odd? Because of Swiss money?" Winifred asked.

"No. That's odd, of course. But the thing that struck me as *really* odd is their name. Apparently they didn't use their real names when they registered with your mother. Their real name, it turns out, is *Willoughby*."

Richie was still at the computer. Winston had given him the correct size, and he had found a toy car wheel on the computer. The company wouldn't sell just one. You had to buy two dozen. He had added them to the shopping cart and was waiting to get credit card information from his father. But now his attention had been caught by the story of the hospitalized tourists.

"Willoughby's *your* name, Dad! And mine!" he said.

"That's right," Tim Willoughby said. "I was twelve when I was adopted by Commander Melanoff, and I decided to keep my last name." He turned to Winifred. "I explained that I was an orphan, didn't I?"

She nodded. But she was becoming very confused.

"Here," he said, handing a credit card to Richie. "This one's still good. I've canceled all the others. Buy the cheapest wheels they have." Richie began to type the numbers in.

"Pay extra to have them delivered overnight. It doesn't cost much more, and this will be our final order; we might as well go down with a flourish," his father instructed. "In the meantime we'll get the car prepared. We'll sand it and repaint it and oil the axles. How does that sound?"

"Great!" Winston and Richie both said.

"Then tomorrow, when the wheels arrive, we'll put four new wheels on it and it'll be as good as new. *Better* than new!"

"Just like when your dad made it for you," Richie said, to Winston. Winston nodded, picked up the car, and held it close to his heart.

Everyone was silent for a moment. Then, suddenly, Richie's father said, "Son, I'm sorry I haven't been a better father."

"It's okay, Dad," Richie told him. "You bought me lots of stuff."

"No, it's not okay. I'm going to try to be better. It's just that—well, I told you I was an orphan."

The children all nodded.

"So I never had a great dad to learn from. I did have a dad once, for a while, till I was twelve, but he never liked me very much. He always called me a dolt. He shortchanged me on my allowance every single week. And—" He stopped talking because he was choked up.

"What's going to happen to the people who threw

up on my sheets?" Winifred asked. She was trying to change the subject because she didn't like it when people burst into tears.

Richie's father cleared his throat. "I told the hospital director that they could come here. We have plenty of room, at least until we have to sell this house. And I didn't know what else to suggest.

"Isn't it extremely odd, though," he mused, "that their name is Willoughby?"

33

So close! Ben Poore thought as he climbed down from the cab of the truck just outside of Seattle. The driver handed his heavy pack down to him and drove away without saying *goodbye* or *good luck*.

Yet the driver had been so close to ordering the encyclopedia! Several hundred miles, Ben had had, to present his sales pitch, so there had been no rush, as there so often was when someone was trying to slam their front door on you. No, this guy had listened, had shown interest, had even asked about the payment plan.

When had it turned bad? He tried to remember. Probably it was when they had stopped at a gas station, hit the men's room, and bought some bad coffee. There had been a picnic table. Yes, it was at the picnic table that things turned sour. The driver, listening in the cab as Ben talked, had shown real interest. So at the rest stop Ben had dumped everything from his pack and laid the sample materials out in order on the rough boards. There was a hardened stain of bird-dropping on the edge of the table, he recalled. He had asked about the driver's family, ascertained that there were children, had begun his talk about the importance of knowledge, how the kids' grades in school would improve if they had access at home to—

The driver had interrupted him. "What're those?" he asked, pointing.

Ben had looked. "Oh, just some souvenirs I'm taking to my kids. Rocks. My little girl's really interested in geology. I mailed her a big box full but I saved these just to bring me luck as I make my way home.

"She and I will be spending a lot of time with the G volume. Or maybe the M, for minerals. How about your kids? What are their hobbies?"

"Can I see them?" The driver had reached for the glistening striated rocks and was turning them over in his hand.

"Maybe they're athletes? Lemme tell you, there's a whole section on the major leagues. My boy's a Yankees fan. But it doesn't matter. All the teams, they're all in there. Well, maybe not the Diamondbacks or the Rays. They're too new."

"You got more of these?" the driver asked.

"Not with me. These are just sample volumes. After I take your order, and your deposit, then the company starts sending them, one volume a month. These are all beat up because I've been traveling. You wouldn't want these. What you'll get will be brand new, for sure."

"I mean the rocks."

"No." Ben Poore reached over and took the rocks back. He dropped them into the backpack. They were distracting the driver.

And he couldn't, no matter how hard he tried as they continued their journey, rekindle the driver's interest. For some reason the driver was fascinated by the rocks.

"You know what? You owe me for gas," the driver said suddenly, as they approached the Canadian-US border. "How about if you just give me those rocks and we'll call it even?"

Ben Poore almost said yes. But instead, he reached into his pocket and pulled out a twenty-dollar bill. It was nearly all the money he had left at the end of his long and unsuccessful year. "Here," he said, and handed it to the driver. Briefly he thought he might offer the rocks as a bonus gift if the guy ordered the encyclopedia. But he decided against it. The driver was becoming annoying. Eventually the silence between them became uncomfortable, vaguely hostile. There was a delay as they went through border control and entered the United States. He tried unsuccessfully to interest the customs agent in an encyclopedia. Finally, as they approached Seattle, he asked the driver to let him out. No need, he thought, to enter a big city. He'd just stand here by the highway on the outskirts and hope for a ride east.

He found himself oddly angry at the rocks. They'd cost him a sale. He reached into the pack past the books and felt for them at the bottom where they lay in a layer of grit and sand. He thought he'd toss them away. They were bad luck.

But at that moment a car slowed and stopped for him. Hastily he rezipped the pack and climbed into the back seat, already beginning to wonder if the middle-aged couple in the front might be interested in buying a wonderful gift for their grandkids. It would boost their IQs.

34

The toy car wheels arrived the next morning, as promised. The Poore children were at the mansion, with Richie, when the UPS truck pulled into the driveway. And there they were: shiny black plastic with hubcaps painted in metallic silver: exactly right, they all decided.

"Can I do it? Can I put the new wheels on?" Richie was holding the little car, now sanded and repainted bright red.

"It's Winston's car, Richie," his father reminded him.

Richie held the toy firmly. "I'll trade you, Winston," he suggested. "How about it? You can have my remote-control Lamborghini!"

But Winston shook his head. "Sorry. But my father made this for me. He started with a block of wood and carved the shape of the car. Remember, Winifred?"

She nodded. "He cut his finger. There was a little bloodstain on the car before he painted over it." She pointed to the underside of the car body, where the bloodstain had been.

"So I can't trade it away. My dad wanted me to have it." Winston reached for the car and Richie relinquished it with reluctance.

"You know what, Richie?" his father said. "We were required to buy—how many was it? Two dozen wheels?"

Richie nodded. Winston had set four wheels on the table and was beginning to screw the first one onto the right side of the car's front axle. The open package lay nearby with the remining wheels encased in polyurethane.

"So there are how many left? Math problem!"

Richie, Winifred, and Winston all groaned together because it was so easy. They answered, in unison, "Twenty!"

"Well, then. Choose four wheels, Rich, and let's find us a block of wood and I'll start carving!"

Richie giggled. "Dad," he said, "you won't be any good at it! You don't even have the right knife!"

His father pointed to Richie's computer. "Take a look and see if there's an inexpensive carving tool. That will be the absolute final thing I buy. I'm closing my last credit card down."

"I'll help." The deep voice was unexpected. But there he was, again, at the playroom door. This time Commander Melanoff was dressed and his thick white hair was combed.

"Do you know how to carve, Grandfather?" Richie asked.

"How do you think the original Easter candies were created? All those bunnies and chicks out of marshmallow? I carved the first designs myself! Right upstairs in the original lab. Had a hard time with the bunny tails, I remember. Marshmallow's not an easy thing to carve. I think it might have been easier if I'd used nougat."

"To think, Commander," Tim Willoughby reminded him sadly, "American children will never experience candy again."

Commander Melanoff was not paying attention. He was reminiscing. "The licorice days; those were the best," he murmured. "Moment of silence, please, for Other Barnaby. He loved Lickety Twist."

Dutifully they all fell silent. Winifred wondered if candy had become illegal in the monastery, too. Did monks have to obey such laws?

"And Nanny was still with us then," Commander Melanoff said, at the end of the silence. He dabbed his eyes. Then he looked up suddenly. "A poem is coming," he announced, and then began to recite:

There once was a woman named Nanny . . .

"Please, not the naughty one, Grandfather," Richie said. Commander Melanoff frowned briefly at him and continued.

Who looked forward to being a Granny . . .

He paused for a moment, deep in thought. "Well," he said, "it's making me too sad to go on."

Richie, still at the computer, announced, "Here! Wood-carving sets. And some of them come with instruction books!"

"Order the very cheapest one, son," Tim Willoughby said, then turned to his adoptive father, who was dabbing his eyes with a handkerchief. "Are you all right, Commander?"

Commander Melanoff sniffed. "I guess so," he said.

"Think about licorice," Winifred suggested.

He brightened. "Ah, those were wonderful days," he said. "The days of licorice! But I had not yet adopted Tim and his siblings. It was so lonely here in the mansion. My son, Other Barnaby, was a very quiet, introverted boy to begin with, and he had gone off to Europe with my wife. And my wife—to be honest, I had never really liked her very much. She was one of those *meticulous* people—she measured my hair and when it was one four-hundredth of an inch too long she insisted I go to the barber because it made her very nervous. And she *labeled* everything, even my underwear. Anyway, she had run off with a postman, and—"

"A postman?" Richie asked. "Like Mr. Shaughnessy, our mailman who wears US Postal Service shorts, even in winter? He likes labels too. He likes when people print address labels because they're easier to read, he says."

"No, no," his grandfather explained. "Not Mr. Shaughnessy. He was probably just a boy during the time I'm talking about. This was all more than thirty years ago. And anyway, my wife ran off with a *Swiss* postman. Actually, a postmaster. His name was something like Hans, or maybe Fritz."

Winston and Winifred spoke in unison. "*The Swiss Postal System*!" they said. "Might Be Distressing!"

"Precisely," said Commander Melanoff. "It was very distressing, because—"

But he was interrupted by the sound of the doorbell.

35

Mrs. Poore rang the doorbell at the mansion in the late afternoon. She had combed her hair and ironed her dress, hoping that perhaps they would invite her to eat with them again, and that once again strawberry shortcake might be on the menu.

But she had another reason to ring their bell.

"I need to see my dear children!" she said, when Richie's mother answered the door. "Look!" She held up a postcard. "I've heard from their father!"

Winston and Winifred, summoned from the playroom, leaned close to their mother and read the message on the postcard that she held out to show them.

Dear Family,
I have not been inebriated in months. I am still depressed, though, because of no $$$. Have not sold a single set of encyclopedias. I am coming home to develop a new sales technique. Bringing souvenirs for all of you: rocks for the win-wins, and a flower for my dearest wife. You can expect me on Saturday if all goes well.

xoxoxo Ben Poore

"When's Saturday?" asked Winifred.

"Day after tomorrow," her brother said.

"And what's *inebriated*?"

"*Inebriated* means having drunk too much alcohol, dear," Mrs. Poore told her daughter. "You remember that now and then your dear father had a tendency to do that."

"But now he doesn't?"

"Yes, it appears that now he doesn't."

"And he's bringing us souvenirs!" Winifred exclaimed.

Winston frowned. *"Rocks?"*

"I love rocks," Winifred reminded him. "Did you know that one single rock can have a whole lot of different minerals in it?"

"And a flower for me!" her mother said. "How romantic! I must remember, though, if it has leaves, not to make a salad from them. It seems to have been the salad that caused the problem for my guests."

"Those strange guests! Does anyone know what happened to them? Did they survive?" asked Winston.

Richie's father had been listening from the foot of the stairs, where he stood with Richie, holding his hand. "They're recovering," he told the Poores, "and I suppose I'd better tell my wife that they're coming here

—she'll be a little upset because we've had to let the maids go. It will probably be Saturday."

"My goodness!" Mrs. Poore said. "The same day my husband returns! Wouldn't it be a lovely idea to have a Welcome Home party for everyone all together? Of course, my little house would be a bit crowded for such an event . . ."

She waited.

"There would be—let me think—the four of us Poores, and Richie and his parents—that's seven—and the guests, whatever their names were . . ."

"*Willoughby*, apparently," Richie's father said.

"Same name as my dad! And me!" Richie said.

"Just a coincidence," his father said.

"Yes, the two of them. That makes nine," Mrs. Poore went on.

"And Grandfather," Richie added. "But he's not a Willoughby."

"That would make ten! A little large for my pathetic kitchen table . . ."

She waited.

Finally she said, "Well, I guess I could have a buffet dinner. Wouldn't that be nice? I don't have ten forks, but people could eat with their hands. I could make a huge salad! I know my previous salad did cause some problems, but—"

Richie's father sighed and interrupted her. "I think it would be wise," he said in a resigned voice, "to do it here."

"Lovely!" said Mrs. Poore. "And perhaps after dinner my husband could do a presentation of his encyclopedias."

36

When the Willoughbys had been moved out of the intensive care unit, when they were no longer in danger of death, they were given a shared private room at the hospital. Although the administration had not been able to figure out how the hospital would be paid for their care, since the mysterious couple seemed to have no insurance and no savings and no income, they realized that there was a value to this unusual pair of patients.

Somehow there had been a leak. Calls from the media were coming in. A lab assistant, overhearing the talk about what the pathology report had revealed—that the couple had been defrosted after many years—had notified the newspapers.

Now the hospital was receiving requests for interviews. A publisher was offering a book contract. Every TV station was eager to do a special, and late-night comedians had begun performing routines about cryogenics (*What happened when the frozen body was thawed and revived? He had to pay ex-ice tax*). A reporter with a camera and digital recorder in his pockets had disguised himself as a janitor and tried to get into the Willoughbys' room with a dustpan and broom. But he had been intercepted. All the calls had as yet been declined. So far the news was not out to the public.

And Mr. and Mrs. Willoughby, though they were feeling better after the unfortunate salad,[1] were beginning to have a lot of difficulty adjusting to the thirty-year gap in their personal history.

"What does that mean: *This Hospital Is a Smoke-Free Zone*?" Mrs. Willoughby said to a nurse's aide who was wheeling her to Radiology for an X-ray on her sore foot. She was reading a sign on the wall of the hallway.

"Just what it says," the attendant explained. "No smoking allowed anywhere."

"Well, that's crazy! What if I wanted to sit down and have a cigarette? Would I have to go out of the hospital and find a restaurant or something?"

The nurse's aide looked at her in amazement. "Restaurants don't allow smoking," she pointed out.

"They *don't?* When did that happen?"

[1] Wouldn't this be a great title—*The Unfortunate Salad*? I'd buy it if I saw it in a bookstore.

The nurse's aide shrugged. "I don't know. Before I was born."

Later, back in the room they shared, Mrs. Willoughby's husband was watching the television that hung on the wall facing their beds. He glanced over when she was wheeled in. "Guess what," she told him. "People can't smoke anywhere anymore."

"I was wondering why there weren't any cigarette commercials," he replied.

"The whole television thing is strange. What are *premium channels*?" his wife said. "What's HBO?"

"Beats me."

She rose from the wheelchair and climbed up into her bed beside his. "My foot's okay," she said. "Just a blister."

"I told you those shoes were trouble."

She sighed. "I know. You were right. I'll have to figure out how to get new ones."

The nurse's aide, who had folded the blanket that had covered Mrs. Willoughby's lap and was about to wheel the chair out to the hall, looked up. "If you know your size, you can get great shoes on Zappos. Just Google Zappos to find the website," she said casually. "See you later. I'll be bringing your dinner in after a bit." Then she left the room.

"What did that girl say?" Mr. Willoughby clicked the TV off with the remote and turned to his wife.

She looked puzzled. "I think she said to Google shoes for Zappos. Or maybe to Zappo shoes for Google?"

"What does that *mean?*"

Mrs. Willoughby put her head in her hands and began to cry. "I have no idea," she said.

Her husband gazed at her for a moment. Then he, too, began to weep. "The news was on TV while you were gone, Frances," he whimpered, "and I understood *nothing*. What is Brexit? Who is Tom Brady? And what is Facebook?"

37

Ben Poore, bearded, with unkempt hair, a backache, dirty fingernails, holes in his shoes, and a big smile, knocked on the door of the little house late Saturday afternoon and was greeted with happy shrieks and enthusiastic hugs. He was so glad to be home and to see his wife and children once again. At the kitchen table he emptied his backpack. The sample encyclopedia volumes came out; he opened one of them and withdrew from between two pages in the middle a dried and flattened flower, which he handed with a flourish to his wife.

"Dwarf fireweed," he told her. "Latin name: *Chamerion latifolium*. I picked it at Mineral Creek."

Mrs. Poore wiped away a few tears. "I think I'm crying for joy," she explained. "Or I might be allergic to dwarf fireweed."

He set the battered sample volumes aside. "These are too messed up from all the travel," he said. "They didn't bring about any sales. I'm sorry I didn't come back with riches for you. You deserve riches, my dear family."

"It's okay, Father," Winston said. "I still have the toy car you made me!"

"And you said you brought us some rocks as souvenirs!" Winifred added. "You know how I love rocks!"

Their father reached into the gritty bottom of the emptied pack, took out the two rocks he'd been carrying for so long, and handed one to each of his Win-Win children.

"Look at the glittery parts! Oh, I wish I had a pocket," Winifred said, scrunching up the fabric of her dress.

"We can't afford pockets," her mother reminded her, "but we should be so grateful that you have a dress. Some little girls don't even have a dress."

Winifred sighed and whispered to her mother, "You're Marming again."

"Sorry."

"It's okay," Winifred said, and placed her rock on the windowsill.

"I have pockets," Winston boasted. "Boys' pants always have pockets! But I'm going to put my rock on the windowsill beside yours. I need my pockets for my toy car."

"I hate to mention this," Mr. Poore said, looking around the kitchen, "but I'm very hungry. I haven't eaten since South Dakota. A nice truck driver bought me a fried chicken dinner in Pierre, South Dakota. Did you know that's pronounced *Peer*? Some people try to pronounce it the French way. But if you have an encyclopedia, you can learn how to pronounce every single capital in the USA."

Mrs. Poore had opened the refrigerator and was moving some containers around.

"Don't let her give you salad," Winston whispered.

"I have leftover gruel," Mrs. Poore said. "But what time is it? Does anyone know?"

No one had a watch. The clock on the kitchen wall had stopped months before; it needed a new battery.

But Mr. Poore opened the back door and went out into the yard, looking up at the sky. "I learned to read the sky in Alaska," he explained. "I have to adjust for time zones, of course, but I'd say five p.m."[1]

"In that case," his wife announced, "I'll save the gruel for breakfast. It's time to go next door. We're invited there for dinner."

[1] We don't exactly know where they live. But I'm guessing northeast USA. Maybe Hartford, Connecticut?

38

It was late in the day by the time Mr. and Mrs. Willoughby were finally officially released from the hospital. They had been ready for hours—dressed, sadly, in wrinkled hospital gowns, with paper slippers on their feet, because their clothing had been so tattered by their travel and then stained by their illness. But they had had to wait while the paperwork was completed, and then for several hours while the hospital administrators figured out a way to deceive the reporters who had been gathered outside the front entrance for days.

Finally a hearse, lengthy and black, pulled up to an unobtrusive back entrance. It had been the clever idea, actually, of Tim Willoughby. He had even suggested placing the couple in matching coffins and carrying them out, but they had balked at that. Instead, two funeral directors, middle-aged men in somber suits, got out of the vehicle and helped the pair, still a little unsteady because of their illness, into the back, where they balanced on cushions and were driven quietly away.

There, in the darkness, Mr. Willoughby put his arm around his wife. "You remember that once I said you looked like a hippo?" he whispered.

She sniffled a bit. "I shouldn't have been insulted," she replied. "I did need to lose a few pounds."

"No, no, it wasn't that at all! What I meant was—and I'm sorry I phrased it so badly—that you looked determined. Resolute. Like someone who sets a goal and then makes her way toward it, overcoming obstacles at every turn, and—"

"Like a—"

"Yes, dearest. Like a hippo. Such a magnificent beast."

"Thank you," Mrs. Willoughby murmured, and grasped his hand. "And I feel that we'll make our way through this difficult situation. It was lovely of Commander Melanoff's family to offer us a stay in their magnificent home while we sort things out."

"I only wish—" her husband began.

"I know. I too wish that we had clothes. These hospital gowns are so silly, and they flap open in the back."

"Actually, dearest," Mr. Willoughby continued, "I was going to say that I am beginning to wish that our children could be with us as things fall into place."

"Yes, our children," Mrs. Willoughby said sadly.

"Them. We probably shouldn't have been so hateful to them." She sniffed. "You always used to call the eldest —I've forgotten his name again—a dolt, remember?"

"Tim. Well, he was doltish at times. Still, he was our firstborn." Mr. Willoughby's voice was wistful.

"We'll just have to put him out of our minds. Let's focus on the future."

From the front seat, one of the two undertakers looked back into the darkened rear of the vehicle and said, "You okay back there? Want me turn on the satellite radio?"

The passengers were silent. "What's a satellite radio?" Mrs. Willoughby whispered to her husband.

"Not a clue," he whispered back. "No thanks!" he called to the driver.

"We'll be there in about ten minutes. You comfortable?"

The two of them, holding hands, maintaining their balance as the hearse rounded a corner, called back that they were doing just fine.

39

Not far away, in the mansion, Mrs. Poore had introduced her husband to Richie and his family.

"I apologize for my informal outfit," Ben Poore said to Commander Melanoff, who was wearing a tuxedo. "I've been on the road for a long time."

"I understand completely," Commander Melanoff replied. "I myself made several sorrowful trips to Switzerland, and each time, coming home I felt unkempt. I do like your plaid shirt, by the way. You look very, ah, rustic."

"Were you hungry, returning from sorrowful trips? I myself have not had a meal since South Dakota." They were standing in the hall, but Ben Poore glanced into the dining room. The kitchen staff, despite the fact that they had been laid off and had no salary forthcoming, had decided out of loyalty to return to the mansion to prepare one final, sumptuous meal. Mr. Poore could see that the long table was lavishly set with a large ham decorated with pineapple slices, and there appeared to be a platter of fried chicken as well, plus several casseroles of macaroni and cheese—and was that perhaps a spinach soufflé? It certainly looked like a spinach soufflé. "I find that I'm a bit hungry. Just a tad." He tried to keep his voice from sounding groany. "Famished, actually," he added, under his breath.

"Indeed, I was often hungry in those days because I was lonely . . . that is, until I met Nanny, who was such a wonderful cook. Do you see her there, on the wall? A handsome woman. And oh my, her seafood casserole, I recall . . ."

Ben Poore choked back a sob. "Seafood casserole?" he moaned. He gazed into the dining room.

"A poem is coming on," Commander Melanoff announced.

"Not the naughty one, Grandfather!" Richie exclaimed. But he was ignored.

There once was a woman named Nanny
Whose skill at the stove was uncanny . . .

There was a loud groan from Ben Poore.

"Is something wrong, Mr. Poore?" Richie's mother asked. "Are you in pain?"

Ben Poore took a deep breath. "No. I'm not in pain.

I'd call it *pangs*, I think. I was just reacting to the word *stove* in that lovely poem, and also noticing a wonderful aroma coming from— I suppose that must be the dining room?"

"Yes, the dining room. But first we'll go into the drawing room, down the hall here, for a brief talk about the history of the Consolidated Confectionaries. Sadly its doors have closed for the last time, but we cherish its memory and want to use this gathering as an opportunity to memorialize its existence. Would you lead the way, children? And perhaps our other guests will arrive soon."

Richie, Winifred, and Winston ran ahead down the long hall, stopping briefly to nod reverently at Nanny's portrait. Then they opened the wide doors to the drawing room. The adults followed them. One of them, Ben Poore, was whimpering.

40

"Commander," said Tim Willoughby, "I have the projector and the screen all set up for you." He turned to the guests and explained, "The commander is going to use PowerPoint.

"I do want to add that we have checked with the authorities, and it is not illegal to display photographs of candy, or to talk about candy."

Everyone (except Ben Poore, who had discovered a small dish of illegal mints on an antique table and had surreptitiously put fourteen of them into his mouth) smiled politely.

"I'll advance the slides, Grandfather," Richie said.

The first photo on the screen was of a simple unwrapped chocolate bar.

"This was my very first confection." Commander Melanoff explained. "Quite simple. Just chocolate—semisweet, if I remember correctly. No nuts or raisins. I created it after a vacation in Mexico, where I learned about the ancient art of chocolate-making. Mayan tombs contained vessels with residue of a chocolate drink dating back to 400 CE."

He advanced to the next photograph, which showed a Mayan tomb.

"We took Richie to Mexico on a vacation when he was a toddler," murmured Richie's mother, "but he didn't display much interest in the museums, I'm afraid. He liked the kiddie pool at our hotel."

"Yes, I remember when dear Winifred was a toddler," Mrs. Poore murmured back. "Of course, we could never afford a vacation. But we had a plastic wading pool in the yard until the cat's claws made it unusable. After that I cut the plastic into rectangles for placemats."

"I know my dad would like to join us on a vacation, if we could afford a vacation," Winston said. "Wouldn't you, Father?" He looked at his father, who had just noticed a bowl of grapes on a nearby table and was trying to sidle his way across the sofa so that he could reach it. His father murmured in agreement that yes, he would like to join his family on a vacation.

"But one archeological site on Mexico's Pacific coast suggests that chocolate beverages may date back to 1900 BCE," Commander Melanoff continued, and nodded to Richie, who clicked on the next picture, which was a chart and a timeline.

Ben Poore groaned slightly, lifted the grapes from the bowl, and filled his mouth.

"The Aztecs adopted cacao into their culture but were not able to grow cacao beans themselves. They valued it so highly that some people paid their taxes in beans. This lovely little statue is of a man carrying a cacao pod. It's in the Brooklyn Museum." Richie advanced to a picture of a primitive stone statue.

"How interesting," Winifred said. "Isn't that interesting, Father?" She looked at Ben Poore, who now had such a large mouthful of grapes that he was unable to speak. "Mmmmm," he mumbled.

The next picture was of a marshmallow bunny posed in an Easter basket.

"I went on, as you know, from those early unadorned chocolates to much more sophisticated confections. Richie, would you just run through some of our most popular items? Please let me know if there are questions about a specific candy, and we can linger."

Ben Poore leaned over and whispered a question to Richie's mother. "Are those real apples in that bowl on the table under the window?" he asked. "Or are they made of wax?"

"Real," she whispered back.

"Excuse me," he said to the people seated around them, and got up and made his way to an antique chair near the window. "Please go on. I'm listening," he assured Commander Melanoff.

Picture after picture appeared. Chocolate bars. Candy eggs decorated with spun sugar. Peppermint sticks. Fudge. The famous licorice sticks known as Lickety Twist. (Everyone said "Awwww" when that photo appeared.)

From the chair by the window, a crunchy noise revealed that Ben Poore had bitten into an apple.

Commander Melanoff straightened his bow tie and adjusted his cummerbund.[1] "To be honest," he added, "my first wife and I were not terribly compatible. I know I've explained that she was a very tidy woman. Nothing wrong with being tidy! But every night she went up to my lab on the third floor, the very lab where I concocted my incredible mixtures as I invented newer and more delectable candies, and she dumped everything out and washed all the containers and tore up my formulas and threw them away. So every morn-

[1] You don't know what a cummerbund is, do you? Better find out before prom time.

ing I had to start all over again. I was actually relieved when she went on vacations without me. It gave me a chance to work without interruption."

"Where did she go on vacations, Grandfather?" asked Richie.

"She went to Europe. Would you run up to your Book Room and bring back the book about the Alps?"

Richie glanced nervously at his mother. "It's MBD," he said.

"Go ahead, dear," his mother said, "if your grandfather is sure he wants you to."

Commander Melanoff nodded to Richie, who left the room. They could hear him dashing up the stairs. In a moment he returned, handed the volume to his grandfather, and took his seat again.

Commander Melanoff opened the book to the center and found a brightly illustrated map. He held the open book up with his finger on the map and walked back and forth in front of his audience so that they could each get a glimpse. "Zermatt," he said. "That's where she went."

From the window seat where he was munching on an apple, Ben Poore announced, "If anyone is interested in more information about Zermatt, I have Volume Z of a wonderful encyclopedia just next door."

"She never got there, actually," the commander said. "That's where she was headed—by private railroad car, incidentally, very luxurious—but along the way . . .

"Richie, would you run back up to your Book Room and bring back the volume about avalanches?"

"Oh dear," murmured Richie's mother. "Are you certain? That's *so* MBD."

Commander Melanoff ignored her, nodded to Richie, and once again they heard his feet pounding up the long staircase. In a moment he was back with the book about avalanches.

"You don't mean to say she was—" Winifred said in a terrified voice.

"Yes, dear. Buried by an avalanche."

"Oh, my! But she managed to be saved?"

"Eventually. But she and our son—"

"Other Barnaby," Richie explained. He looked around. "Moment of silence?" he suggested.

They all fell silent for a brief moment. Then Commander Willoughby continued: "They stayed in the small village where they had emerged, and she met the postmaster, who was just as tidy as she was—everything had to be alphabetical, of course, in the post office—just as orderly, and eventually I got word that our marriage had ended and she was becoming Mrs. Hans. Or maybe it was Mrs. Fritz."

Richie's father stood up. "But then you met Nanny—"

"There once was a woman named Nanny," Commander Melanoff said in a reverent voice. *"Who had an incomparable—"*

Tim interrupted him. "An incomparable skill in the kitchen! I remember crème caramel for dessert!"

Ben Poore shot up from his chair. "What did I just hear?" he asked. "Did someone say *crème caramel*?"

"Let's make our way to the dining room," Richie's mother said, rising from the sofa. "We won't wait for our other guests. It appears that they'll be late."

As they all began walking toward the dining room, Winifred made her way to Commander Melanoff and took his hand. His story had made her terribly sad.

"I'm so sorry your wife was in an avalanche," she said. "That's why the book about avalanches MBD: must be distressing."

He looked down at her in surprise. "Oh, goodness, no," he said. "It's true that avalanches are distressing. But my wife survived, and I was thrilled that she decided not to return. I only wish she had not taken on the task of reorganizing the Swiss postal system. It made it almost impossible to ship my licorice candies to Switzerland. I ended up with a whole shipload of Lickety Twist held hostage in Rotterdam for months."

"Goodness!" said Winifred. "That—"

Commander Melanoff finished her sentence as they entered the dining room. "Yes," he said, "indeed. Very MBD."

"And now it's all illegal anyway," Winifred said sadly.

"Wait a minute!" Winston spoke in a loud voice. "I've been thinking a lot about this while my sister has been thinking about minerals, which do not interest me in the slightest. I'm really interested in machinery. And while we were watching the presentation about Consolidated Confectionaries, I thought about the vats and the compressors and the label-makers and the robots, and the flavor dispensing machine— Do you still have the flavor-dispensing machine, Mr. Willoughby?"

"Of course," Tim Willoughby said. "We'll be auctioning everything off, now that the factory has closed."

"Not so fast," Winston said. "You can repurpose it all! Just think about it! Every night, every morning, what does every one of us do? We go into our bathrooms and we . . . what?"

Richie giggled. "That's inappropriate," he said.

Winston winced. "I *meant*," he explained, "that we all brush our teeth."

Everyone nodded.

"And," Winston went on, "what if we had toothpaste that tasted like the one wonderful taste we remembered from the past?"

"Lickety Twist," Commander Melanioff murmured.

"Exactly! It will be so easy to convert the machinery so that it uses the same flavoring, puts it into paste, squishes it into tubes, and there you have it! And we'll call it . . ."

He waited. No one replied.

"Lickety Spit!"

The entire room burst into spontaneous applause.

Richie's mother had heard a noise outside and had gone to the front door. She returned to the room looking very concerned. "Tim," she said, to her husband, "there's a vehicle pulling into the driveway. It looks like a hearse!"

41

Two hours later, finally, after chaos, confusion, consternation, and at last pecan pie with vanilla ice cream all around, everyone was once again in the drawing room. But there were two more people now, dressed in hospital garments that came to their knees and tied in the back with a good deal of unfortunate flapping-open. They sat on the velvet-tufted sofa, on either side of Tim Willoughby, who looked stunned. His arms were around them both. "Father!" he kept saying. "Mother!"

Henry Willoughby handed his son Tim an envelope. "This is all crumpled," he said apologetically. "It was in my pants pocket when we went to the hospital. And now my pants are kaput. I'm afraid I barfed on them. All I have is this ridiculous hospital gown with no pockets, but—"

"I'll find you some clothes," Tim said. "We're about the same size. And for you too, Mother. I know we have Nanny's clothing packed away."

"Anything but *brown,*" Mrs. Willoughby said.

Henry Willoughby interrupted his wife and indicated the envelope. "I kept that throughout the hospitalization," he said to Tim. "It's an official statement."

"Please," Tim said. "Let's not discuss statements. I've been reading too many discouraging bank statements lately."

"That will change," his father said. "And this is a different kind of statement."

"What is it, Dad?" asked Richie, looking at the sealed envelope in Tim's hands.

"I don't know. Let me open it." Tim tore open the envelope and withdrew a colorful card with a handsome picture of a horse with his mane flowing. "*I'm sorry . . .*" he read aloud.

"I looked for anything but bunnies or flowers," Henry Willoughby explained.

Tim opened the card to reveal the other end of the horse, with its tail swishing away flies. ". . . *I've been a you-know-what,*" he read.

Richie leaned over to see the card more clearly. "You've been a horse's tail?" he asked Henry Willoughby.

"I have. I was a bad dad. I didn't pay enough attention to my children."

"I have a great dad," Richie said happily. He stroked his father's arm.

Tim Willoughby put his arm around his little boy. "You realize," he said to the couple in the hospital gowns, "this is your grandson?"

They looked startled for a moment. "But we're not old enough to have—" Frances Willoughby began. "Or maybe we are? I can't figure any of this out!"

"And that reminds me," said her husband. "We had other children! What about the twins? And—oh, dear—what has become of little Jane?"

"All grown up," Tim explained. "Successful. Happy. Tell you what! We'll go upstairs to the computer after we finish our coffee and we'll FaceTime them all. You'll be amazed to see Jane. She has tattoos."

"Do Skype, Dad!" Richie suggested.

"What's FaceTime?" asked Henry Willoughby. "What's Skype?"

Commander Melanoff had been putting away the projector he had used for his PowerPoint presentation. He looked up suddenly. "You know," he said, "I remember when your accident happened. I was actually subscribing to some Swiss newspapers, because not long before, my wife had decided to take up with the Swiss postmaster. Not that that was in the news! But my attention was caught by an article about how two Americans had decided to climb a Swiss mountain peak—"

"Alp," said Mr. Willoughby. "It was an Alp."

"Yes, yes, of course," the white-haired man went on, "but the Americans didn't have the proper clothing or equipment. I'm sorry, but the reporters all said that—"

"We had *crampons*," Mrs. Willoughby said. "It was just that we didn't know how to wear them. I blame L.L.Bean. Is that where we bought the crampons, dear? From L.L.Bean?"

"No, I think it was some other company. But it was definitely their fault. They didn't tell us how to wear them."

"I thought they looked nice on our heads, though, didn't you, dear?" She reached over and took his hand.

"You know what?" Tim Willoughby said. "I think that you two, at least in the realm of mountain climbing, were *dolts*."

Henry Willoughby looked shocked. "That's a terrible thing to say to your father!" Then he paused. "But I used to say it to you, didn't I, Tim?"

"You did. All the time."

"Can you forgive me?"

"Of course," said Richie's father.

"You know what?" Winston said. "You should have Googled crampons. Or looked on YouTube. I bet anything there's a YouTube video showing how to use crampons."

Mrs. Willoughby stood up suddenly. Then, when she realized that her backside was exposed, she sat back down. Still, she spoke in a loud voice. "That's *it!*" she said. "I am so tired of all this Googling and YouTubing and FaceTiming and Zappo-ing or whatever it is, and Instagram and—*Skype?* What on earth is *that?* Henry, we missed out on everything while we were frozen! It's not fair! What on earth is Twitter? And I have no *shoes!*" She began to cry.

Mr. Willoughby reached over and patted her hand. But he too looked a little frustrated and weepy.

Their son Tim tried to reassure them. "Mother," he said, though the word felt a little awkward to him, "don't worry about any of that. It will all fall into place."

"We'll make the best of it," Mrs. Poore murmured.

"What does that *mean*, exactly?" asked Winifred, but no one responded.

"But look at me!" Mrs. Willoughby wailed. "I'm younger than my son is!"

Her husband suddenly leaned forward, closer to her. "Frances," he said, "even without my glasses, I think I see some wrinkles starting in your neck! A little like—what's that wrinkly dog—a shar-pei? You look a little like that! It could be that you are actually starting to age!"

"You think?" She calmed a little. "I hope not too fast."

Winifred, who'd been listening, said to Richie's father, "Mr. Willoughby, there's a book on the MBD stack about orphans. But you're not an orphan anymore! Your parents are alive!"

"So is my ex-wife," Commander Melanoff pointed out. "She and her husband have retired from the post office. They're very old now. But when we were all younger, Nanny and I . . ." He paused. *"There once was a woman named Nanny . . ."* he recited wistfully.

"No, Commander," Tim said gently, and patted his hand. "Not now."

"Incomparable." The old man bit his lip. "Well. Anyway. Nanny and I would go to visit them now and then, in their Swiss village. It was quite boring, actually."

"There's an MBD book about the Swiss postal system! I'm going to go and get that whole stack of books and we'll . . . I don't know, throw them in the fireplace or something!" Winifred left the drawing room and they all chuckled as once again they heard a young person's feet thundering up the stars.

In a minute she was back, and breathless. But she was holding only one book, and a magnifying glass.

"That's not MBD," Winston pointed out. "That's the book about—"

"Right! Geology! I'd left it there on the chair where I'd been reading. When I saw it, I suddenly remembered—" She began turning the pages of the thick book. "Tellurium, calaverite, let me see . . . Winston?"

"What?" her brother glanced over from the little toy car with the new wheels that that he'd been showing his father.

"Run over to our house, would you, and get those rocks that Father brought us? They're on the windowsill in the kitchen."

"Oh, all right. But you owe me." Winston left the room.

"I'd go," Winifred said, "but it's urgent that I find the page I'm looking for. Krennerite? I wonder if those shiny streaky things in the rocks . . . ? Could it possibly be . . . ? Father, when you were in Alaska, were you in *gold-mining* territory?"

"I guess I was. But no one wanted to buy a set of outdated encyclopedias." Ben Poore said sadly. He glanced over at the fruit bowl. Amazingly, he was still slightly hungry.

"What do you mean, *outdated?*" Henry Willoughby asked. He leaned forward, adjusting his hospital gown carefully over his knees.

Mrs. Poore explained. "They're thirty years old. So there's nothing in them about artificial intelligence, or about, let me think, or— What else is missing, Winifred?"

"Gluten intolerance. Gene therapy. Global warming. The whole G volume is a mess, it's so outdated."

"Probably no *Google* in it, then?" Mrs. Willoughby asked.

"Oh my, no, I think not," said Mrs. Poore.

Winifred agreed. "No Google. And the V volume is horrible. It still has vampires, and Queen Victoria. But there's nothing about vaping, or Verizon Wireless, or—"

Winston reentered the room, carrying the two rocks. He handed them to his sister. "Here. And the mailman left a big package on the porch. From you, Father. You mailed it from Alaska. It's really heavy."

"More rocks," Ben Poore explained. "Lots more."

"I want one," Henry Willoughby announced loudly.

"I'm afraid not, Mr. Willoughby," Winifred said politely. "Our dad sent them to me all the way from Alaska. They're mine." She picked up her magnifying glass.

"I didn't mean the rocks. I meant the outdated encyclopedias. I want one. I want *two*. More than two! I want all you have. Tim? Son? You haven't spent all my money, have you? There's some left?"

"There's some left. It's in the bank. I didn't need your money because I'd inherited Consolidated Confectionaries. Of course, now that—"

"Just make out a check to Mr.— What's the name again? Penniless? Write a check to Mr. Penniless."

"It's Poore, Dad. His name is Poore."

"I want to read about what the world was like before we were frozen. I want to provide them to the schools! Everyone should know what it was like! Write a check to Mr. Poore and buy every single outdated encyclopedia he has."

Ben Poore looked up. His mouth was full. He had found a lovely ripe peach in the fruit bowl. "Someone wants to buy my—?"

Winifred set down her magnifying glass. In a quiet voice she said, "We don't really need the money anymore. These rocks are gold nuggets. They really truly are. Father? Guess what! You struck gold!"

Her father wasn't listening. He was looking around the table at what food remained. "Does anyone else want those last grapes?" asked Ben Poore. They all shook their heads no, and with a happy sigh he reached for them. "Probably a good thing that candy's disappeared," he said. "Fruit is so much better for you." He popped a grape into his mouth.

Tim Willoughby looked up. He had taken his pen from his pocket and been adding figures on a pad of paper. "In any case," he said, "if they decide to reinstate candy someday, by then we'll have the toothpaste production up and running. By my calculations, we could produce Lickety Twist and Lickety Spit simultaneously, maybe even package them together? You think? I'm picturing a commercial in which a kid munches on a piece of licorice, makes his teeth turn all black, so he gives a funny grin—maybe we'd use a laugh track there—then he goes into the bathroom, picks up his toothbrush, and—" He paused, then picked up the pen again. With a contented look, he scribbled a few more figures.

Winifred stood up. She picked up the small knife that her father had used to peel his peach and tapped it on a glass until everyone had stopped talking and was paying attention to her.

"I just realized what *making the best of it* means!" she said. "This is the best of it. *This!*" She gestured around the room, at all the gathered people who were talking and smiling. "The absolute best."

Then she grinned. "Oops. I think I just Marmed," she said.

In the hallway, looking down from the gold frame at her newly large and very happy family, Nanny seemed to be smiling.

THE END